THE COWBOY BILLIONAIRE'S LUCKY BREAK

KISSING OAKS BILLIONAIRE BROTHERS
BOOK ONE

SYLVIA MCDANIEL

The Billionaire Needs a Fake Engagement.

Since he struck it big with the Powerball, Adrian Landry has been dodging women. Only problem is that he needs an escort for the rodeo ball season, one without any expectations. And when he gets what he wants, it backfires on him, big time.

Accomplished lawyer Madison Benton yearns to return home to Oakdale, Texas, and abandon her high-powered career. When she learns of Adrian's predicament, she proposes a deal. She will be his date for the season if he assists her start-up legal firm. No strings attached.

Is it possible for two people to pretend to be engaged without becoming emotionally attached? Particularly when they've been friends forever.

Sign up for my new book release newsletter and receive a free book! Click Here!

Kissing Oaks Billionaire Brothers

The Cowboy Billionaire's Lucky Break?
The Cowboy Billionaire's Fate
The Cowboy Billionaire's Playbook
The Cowboy Billionaire's Secret
The Cowboy Billionaire's Deception
The Cowboy Billionaire's Match

CHAPTER 1

Adrian Landry knew he should have brought a date to the Burnett's roundup ball. Since his divorce two years ago, women seemed to think he was an open target – a billionaire in need of companionship. And Norma Jean Radcliffe had set her sights on him. All night she'd been flirting, buying him drinks, and laying her hands on him.

Problem was he knew her type of woman and wanted nothing to do with her. And yet, his manners insisted that he not act rude.

There was safety in numbers, so he did his best to remain in a crowd of men, talking cattle, horses, rodeos, and the current price of beef on the hooves.

The man next to him snickered. "Adrian, you're one lucky son of a bitch."

"Yes, I am," he admitted, wondering what brought this up.

Five years ago, Adrian won the Powerball. As a broke, *about-to-lose-his-ranch* cowboy, he'd stopped at a convenience store, and on a whim, bought a ticket. At the time, he'd thought why the hell not?

The next day when he heard on the news that someone in Callahan County had won the Powerball, he remembered he'd purchased a ticket. To his complete disbelief, he discovered the one little stop had changed his life forever.

First, he made the Kissing Oaks Corporation. Then he'd informed his brothers they were all going to college. They wouldn't receive their part of the money until they held a college diploma in their hands.

Next, he'd paid off the debts the ranch had incurred and even brought in a man to help him make the Kissing Oaks Ranch successful. And the man had helped him turn their inheritance into one of the richest spreads in Texas, right up there with the Burnett Family Ranch.

Finally, he'd let Laurie Brown convince him they were ready to marry. It seemed logical, but sometimes logical and practical didn't go together. And love? He'd been fooled by that emotion.

Now he knew better than to believe in that nonsense.

"Why am I lucky?" he asked the man.

"First, you win the Powerball, and next you have beautiful women throwing themselves at you."

"That's not luck," a man standing next to him in a custom tuxedo that looked like western wear said. "That's the power of money. Women can smell a rich man a hundred miles away. Adrian, here, is covered in the scent and they're on the hunt to catch him any way they can."

Adrian laughed. "You're right. I've already been caught once. She hooked me big time. But I'm older and wiser and way more jaded now. Once burned, twice shy."

The men nodded.

"Yes, but the sweet perfume of money is a potent attraction," the man in the tuxedo said. "Look at the gaggle of women standing over there staring at you. You're a wanted man."

Adrian was about to walk away. He didn't like to talk about his personal life or be the center of attention, and since he'd won the lottery, people tried to attach themselves to him. It was hard to know if people were his friends or just lured by the money they knew he had.

"Saw your interview in the Rancher's Magazine," Travis Burnett said. "Good information."

"Thank you," he replied, remembering how the reporter kept asking questions about his personal life and how he'd side-stepped most of them.

"Sorry to hear about you and Laurie," Joshua Burnett said.

What could he say? His ex-wife had found she didn't like being married to a cattleman. She'd expected a life of luxury and traveling the world in a private jet. But he had a ranch to run. A business. He was determined to be successful. And that meant working long hours.

So she'd found refuge in another man's arms.

Half a million dollars later, she was out of his life for good. But now he was back on the meat market and women wanted to latch onto him and drag him to the altar.

One thing Laurie did was make him very aware of how easy it would be to fall prey to a pretty face and a woman's well-rounded curves.

"Thank you. But what these women don't realize is that I'm off the marriage market. I'm done."

The men chuckled.

"How many of you have ever said that?" Mr. Smartass in a

tux asked. "I've certainly said it a number of times and then a pretty woman walks by and I'm a goner."

Cameron Burnett shook his head. "I've watched my cousins meet women and fall in love. As for me, I'm trying to build my own business. I'm looking to find a piece of property and turn it into a place where people can spend their vacation time. Sort of an exclusive B&B for the wealthy."

Tuxedo man shook his head. "Don't you Burnett's own enough of that market?"

"No, we cater to families. This would be for wealthy people. An adult getaway. Not families. A specialty western wedding venue. Weddings are big money."

The men were silent for a moment and Adrian was just about ready to tell them all goodnight when the tuxedo man started to laugh.

"Look out, Adrian, Norma Jean is headed this way with a determined glint in her eyes," he said, smiling. "Damn, I'd like a taste of her."

Adrian was really starting to dislike this guy and even wondered why he was here. But Adrian was networking and had made several lucrative deals with men he'd met at these events. This was business. Not personal. Yet the man's comment was uncalled for.

"Excuse me, gentlemen," Norma Jean said with a purr, dark lashes flickering over her brown eyes focused on Adrian. A pouty smile filled her full lips. "Adrian, would you dance with me?"

His mother, God rest her soul, had taught him to be a gentleman to all women. And as much as he didn't want to, he couldn't turn down Norma Jean's request in front of everyone.

"Yes, ma'am," he said, setting his drink on a tray. After this, he was leaving. He'd had enough for one evening. Time to go home to the quiet, soothing sounds of cattle.

Taking her into his arms, he swept her onto the floor to a waltz.

"How long have you been divorced," she asked him as they glided around the floor to the sounds of the band.

"Two years," he said.

She nodded and he realized she knew how long he'd been divorced. She was just laying the trap that he was certain she was about to spring on him.

"How long since you've been with a woman," she asked her voice a velvety purr.

A bear trap. And if he wasn't careful, he'd get caught.

How did he respond to that brazen question? It had been way too long, but he wasn't about to give in now. Not to the man snare she was setting out.

"Darling," he said with a low throaty growl, "where are you going with this question?"

She gave a little pout. "You're lonely, I'm lonely. We're two adults with needs. We can satisfy each other's desires."

There was no doubt she could satisfy him and probably half the men in the room, but he wasn't going to let his baser needs overtake his better judgment. She'd been around the block a time or two, and he was not going to be her next victim.

He twirled her on the dance floor, maneuvering them around other couples to the sound of the music. "I'm sure that any man in this room would love for you to make that offer to him. But I'm not available."

It wasn't a complete lie. He wasn't available emotionally or physically to any woman. That tap had been turned off.

"Oh, you're seeing someone? I hadn't heard."

Now he would have to lie.

"Yes," he said, thinking maybe he should hire an escort service for a woman to go with him to the balls coming up. It was the beginning of the rodeo season. Tonight was the first gala, and he wasn't looking forward to turning down a woman each time.

A frown crossed her face. "Adrian, I have admired you from afar for years, and after waiting for your divorce to be over and for you to become available, I learn that you've already been snatched up."

Not really, but it was all right. Besides, he remembered her turning up her nose at him when he was a struggling rancher with little to no money. It was only now, post-wealth, that she had taken an interest in him.

It was a big temptation to remind her of how she'd ignored him until she learned he'd won the lottery. But again, he could hear his mother's voice reminding him to be polite regardless of how other people acted.

"Darling, I'm no catch. Just ask Laurie. I couldn't make her happy," he said.

She ran her hand up his chest, her fingers trailing along his muscles. "Some women are stupid. You would make me very happy."

A marriage took two people, and as much as he didn't want to admit it, he'd caused a fair number of problems that sent Laurie running into another man's arms. At the time, he'd been going to college, learning from the man he hired to run the ranch, and determined to make the Kissing Oaks Ranch the best.

In the end, his hard work had been rewarded.

"And some men are just cruel," he said, doing his best to discourage her from acting like a fool for him.

A grin spread across her face. "Honey, a woman like me can tame a cruel man. When I'm finished with you, you'll be begging me for more. You'll be a kitten waiting for me to stroke you."

Damn!

What happened to letting the man pursue a woman? Even if he was interested, her actions were turning him off.

Thankfully, the music came to an end. Like a gentleman, he escorted her from the dance floor, his hand on the small of her back as he guided her toward the side.

Spinning around, she faced him.

"I don't know who you're seeing but drop her. I'll make it worth your while. You won't regret being with me," she said as she leaned in close to his ear. "My pussy is tight and my tongue is wicked."

Did the woman really believe that was going to entice him into spending the night with her? If he was going to attend any more balls, he had to do something to keep the vultures at bay. And he really needed to go to these events if he wanted to keep abreast of the ever-changing ranching business and valuable connections.

When they were off the dance floor, she leaned in and pressed her body into his, and he smelled the sweet perfume she wore. His dick hardened and she grinned, knowing what she was doing to him. It was a natural reaction to a beautiful woman, but nothing more.

At the moment, he felt nothing for this woman, except maybe contempt.

"Honey, follow me home and I'll take care of that for you. Whoever your mystery woman is, she's not doing her job. That would never be a problem if you were my cowboy."

This was not how he wanted a woman. Two years ago, he'd given up his dreams of a wife and family. Two years ago, his wife had broken his heart and ended his hopes and dreams of a happy marriage like his parents.

This was not how he'd ever imagined his wife would act. Norma Jean was not the woman he wanted sharing his bed at night or day. Laurie had ruined him from ever finding a happily ever after.

He leaned in close to her. "Darling, you can quit trying so hard. It's not going to happen."

A red flush filled her face and her sapphire eyes flashed angrily and she grabbed his bolero and pulled him in close. "No man tells me no." She reached down and rubbed her hand on his cock, even though they were in a crowded room. "Sooner or later, you'll say yes. They all do."

She released him and smiled. "Goodnight, Adrian."

With a swish of her silk evening gown, she turned on her stilettos and walked away, her hips swaying with an open invitation.

People stood in small groups talking, and hopefully, no one had noticed that she'd done her best to persuade him to spend the night with her.

Standing speechless, he watched as she walked away, telling his cock to stand down. For the next ball, he'd have to do something different. Anything to help him ward off the vipers like Norma Jean.

CHAPTER 2

*M*adison Benton pushed her long blonde hair away from her face and listened to the real estate agent explain the terms of the lease.

"This space is right on Main Street and you'd have not only foot traffic, but also phone traffic. We only have one attorney in town. You'd be the second. You would be in the center of our small town."

The time had come to move back to her hometown of Oakdale. At the age of seventy, her mother was beginning to have health problems, though she continued to work. Plus, Madison was tired of living in the overcrowded, sprawling city of Dallas. Yes, she was fortunate that she worked with one of the largest law firms in the state, but she longed for her own practice.

She longed to return to small-town living.

The man droned on and on about the little city of Oakdale, and she'd grown up here. She'd graduated from high school and went to Baylor three hours away. But at the age of twenty-nine, she wanted to be closer to her mother to help if she needed anything.

After her mother had a minor stroke, Madison decided it was time to go home. It hadn't been a hard decision when she realized the time had come. Her mother nor she had any idea where her father had gone or if he was dead or alive. And frankly, she didn't care. The two women had done fine on their own.

And now all she needed was ten small clients or one large one for her private practice to make it. And she knew one person who could help her. They'd been friends for years, but she seldom saw him since he'd won the lottery.

Still, maybe he would help her.

"I'll take it," she said, knowing it would be at least a month or longer before she could move in and work permanently from this location. First, she had to finish up a big case she was on, then give her notice before she moved back to where she'd grown up.

"Great. Let's go back to the office and sign the contracts," the man said with a smile.

Afterward, she would visit her mother and tell her the good news. She was coming home.

Failure was not an option, but if she didn't have enough clients within a year, she'd have to make some hard decisions about returning to the city. But for now, she could live off her savings.

An hour later, she got in her Jeep Wrangler Sport and unsnapped the top to let the sunshine in even though it was late January. Yes, it wasn't a glamorous vehicle, but it was a lot of fun. She'd gone off-roading with it, taken it to Colorado, and even to the beach on the National Seashore on Padre

Island. The jeep had been her first major purchase out of college and she loved her vehicle.

Strapping in, she backed out of the real estate office lot and hurried out of town. Fifteen miles later, she turned down the road that led to the Kissing Oaks Ranch. It had changed so much since Adrian won the lottery. He'd made significant improvements, adding security and a very distinct iron gate with the silhouette of a tree.

The Kissing Oaks tree.

She stopped at the intercom and pressed the button. A camera swung in her direction. "Hi, Roger. It's me Madison. I'm here to see my mother."

"Sure, Miss Benton. I'll open the gate for you."

The gate swung open and she hurried on down the road. Years ago, the ranch had been nothing, but now a brand-new fancy house sat at the end of the lane. Since her mother's stroke, Madison had been trying to get her parent to retire, but she loved living out here. After working for the Landry brood for over twenty years, she considered them family.

"Who will cook for them?" she had said when Madison mentioned retirement.

"They're rich; they'll find someone," Madison told her, but her mother refused.

Frankly, Madison didn't care. They were grown men, and yet her mother loved taking care of the six guys who were scattered about the ranch. The men's mother and father had passed away over ten years ago when Adrian was only eighteen, a senior in high school.

She pulled around to the back of the house closer to the kitchen area. After parking the car, she leaped out. It was

Sunday evening and she planned on returning to Dallas tonight.

As Madison rushed into the house, her mother met her at the door.

"Madison, I didn't know you were coming today," she said giving her a hug.

"I told you, Mom," she said, hoping this didn't mean that her mother was getting dementia. "What smells so good?"

"Oatmeal cookies," she said. "Adrian has been moping around today, so I made his favorite cookies hoping to cheer him up."

Maybe this wouldn't be a good time to speak to him after all. But all he could do was say no. But she needed him to say yes.

"What's wrong with him?"

"A good housekeeper minds her own business," her mother said, taking the cookies out of the oven. "What are you doing here?"

That same rule didn't apply to her daughter.

The kitchen door swung open. "Do I smell cookies?"

It wasn't Adrian but Blake his brother.

"She's just taking them out of the oven," Madison replied.

Her mother took a spatula and plated the snacks. Madison and Blake reached for one. She popped the delicious sweet in her mouth. Her mother was an excellent cook.

As the smell drifted through the house, the brothers began to congregate in the kitchen. Finally, Adrian appeared.

"Oatmeal cookies," he exclaimed. "You are supposed to be resting."

"A body can only lie around so much before it turns to stone. Plus, I got bored."

Never once did her mother mention the real reason she'd made the cookies.

"Good to see you, Madison," Adrian said, glancing at her. "I'm not letting your mother do much around the house."

Madison's brows lifted and she shook her head. "Do you really think you could stop her?"

"No, but I'm trying," he said.

Madison couldn't ask for anything more than a caring employer for her aging parent. Well, maybe one more thing.

"Heard you walked away from Norma Jean last night," Garth, the youngest of the six brothers, said.

Adrian sighed. "How in the hell do you learn this stuff?"

Garth laughed. "Facebook. It was filled with pictures of the ball and the two of you dancing. And then someone posted that you were still available. That you had walked away from her."

The man growled. "No, I'm not available. No girlfriend. No dates. Nada. These women are so eager to catch a man with money. Once you receive your inheritance, you'll have the same problem." Picking up another cookie, he gazed at it longingly. "Before the next ball, I'm calling a professional service to send someone over."

His brothers roared with laughter. "Wait until that gets out. Adrian Landry resorts to hiring women."

That wouldn't be good. Not at all.

"Is it wrong to just want a woman to take to functions and nothing else?"

"No, women expect more," his youngest brother said. "You're a catch, and they have their hook, line, and sinker out trying to reel you in."

It was easy to see that could be a problem.

Then an idea struck her. For a moment, she let it roll around in her brain looking at it from all angles. She could help him, and he could help her.

"The season is just getting started," Dakota, one of the twins, said. He and Evan looked so much alike, it was hard to tell them apart, except that Evan was so devilish and loved to create trouble.

"Yes, that's why I need a permanent, non-committed date. An escort. No attachments. No strings, just a good time."

Taking a deep breath, Madison gazed at him. "I could help you."

All heads turned simultaneously toward her, including her mother's.

"We're friends. Nothing more. I'm in the process of opening my own law practice here in town," she said as her mother gasped. "I need clients for it to be successful. You let me handle some of your legal affairs, send me five clients, and I'll pretend to be your girlfriend, your fiancée, whatever it is you need. No emotional attachments. Once the party season is over, we break up."

The kitchen was silent as she gazed into the deepest dark brown eyes. Funny, she'd never noticed that about him before. They'd grown up together, attending the same schools, but she'd lived in town while his family had their ranch.

"Madison, when did you decide to open your own office here?" her mother asked.

"I've been wanting to get out of Dallas for quite some time. When you had the stroke, I decided it was time. Today, I rented an office in downtown Oakdale. In less than two months, I hope to be living here and working in my own place full-time."

Adrian had not responded to her offer.

She glanced at him. "If you don't want to, you don't have to do this. But while you were talking, I thought we could help one another. I'm not after your money. I just want to move back to Oakdale and be close to Mom and run my own practice. And Lord knows I don't want a man, even a rich one. You men are nothing but trouble."

After her college sweetheart and her father's indiscretions, she'd given up on trusting men.

Shaking his head, a smile crossed Adrian's face. "Do you have any idea what you're getting yourself into? Norma Jean is a mean bitch and she's determined that I'm going to be hers. Plus, half a dozen other women like to throw themselves at me. It's this way every time I attend these things."

She wasn't afraid of the blonde bombshell. In fact, they'd not gotten along in school. She'd been a real bitch to Madison.

"I'm not afraid of her. In school, I slapped the fire out of her for being a bully. There is only one way to deal with people like her, and I know just how to put her in her place. And no, it won't be a catfight."

A grin spread across Dakota's face. "Damn, this could get interesting."

"Not really," she replied. "In law school, you learn how to handle difficult people."

"I want to go to the next ball," Garth, the youngest, said.

"No," they all said at once.

Madison knew better than to push him to make a decision. She sank onto a barstool in the kitchen and took another cookie.

"Honey, you don't have to move here for me," her mother said. "I'm fine."

Yes, she was partly moving there to be with her mom, but she also wanted out of the big city.

"Mom, this is what I've been wanting for the last two years. But first, I had to get some experience under my belt. Now seems like the perfect opportunity."

Reaching across the plate, Adrian tried to take the cookie from her.

"What are you doing?"

"If you're going to be my fiancée and go to the dances with me, you don't need to gain weight or you won't fit in your formal. Besides, I love these cookies. I want them all."

She put the cookie to her lips. "One of the rules of me attending is that you will furnish my ball gowns and I can weigh whatever I want. So if I gain five pounds from Mother's cooking, you're not saying one word about it."

A grin spread across his face and he reached into his pocket and pulled out his billfold. Pulling out a thousand dollars, he handed it to her. "Is that enough for a retainer?"

"It's plenty. Next weekend, I think you should take me to dinner. That way, it won't be a total shock when we show up together."

"All right," he said. "Where do you want to go?"

"To the country club, of course. There we'll get the most tongues talking about us."

He nodded. "I'll let you handle all new contracts. Right now, I'm working on two more for cattle sales and three for new construction. Oh, and you'll have to sign a nondisclosure agreement. Whatever is said and done when we're together is private. No sharing on social media."

She nodded.

"Expect to show everyone you're off the market," she said,

knowing it would be important for people to see they were a couple.

With a shake of his head, he sighed. "All right, but just until we get the gold diggers put out to pasture. At the end of the ball season, we're over."

"Agreed," she said.

Elation filled her. She'd gotten everything she'd wanted, plus a few new dresses.

Sliding off the stool, she hugged her mother.

"Where are you going?"

"I've got to find someplace to live," she said. "And I need to write my resignation letter to the firm."

Everything was coming together just like she'd planned. Hurrying out the door, she climbed into the jeep, then Adrian came out the door.

"One more thing. I'm not sleeping with you," he said.

She laughed. "Good. This is a business arrangement. Nothing more. See ya."

CHAPTER 3

In some ways, Adrian felt like he was dating his sister, but he would never let his sister out of the house wearing the dress that Madison wore tonight.

Damn, but when she stepped out of her mother's quarters, his mouth had dropped open and he'd stared at her. The dress fit her figure, showing off her full breasts and small waist. And the heels she wore just made her legs look like they went on forever.

Her blonde hair was swept up off her neck, with a few twirls around her face. Blue eyes with long lashes that hinted at laughter or seriousness. And the woman was smart. She'd graduated at the top of their high school class with a full-ride scholarship to Baylor.

Why was she still single?

"Damn," Blake said. "When did you grow up?"

She laughed. "I'm almost twenty-nine. Where have you been?"

He laughed. "Weren't we out playing rescue the princess just yesterday?"

The princess that wore pigtails and was skinny and they knew threw a mean right hook. Madison was not someone you wanted to get into a fight with at that age.

Those were the fun days. The days of playing outside without a care in the world until your mother called and said it was time for supper and baths.

But this version of Madison was all grown up. Why had he never looked at her like a woman before today?

Even though they had seen each other when she came to visit her mother, he'd never really looked at her like he was seeing her tonight. And tonight's version had his chest aching while he tried to breathe.

"Let's go," he said. "Time to make the Oakdale country club believe we're dating."

"Are you going to kiss her?" Evan asked, grinning.

He would be the one to make this uncomfortable. Already, he could see the mischief on his brother's face, and knew if they didn't leave, it was soon going to be very embarrassing.

"Yes," she said. "No one will believe we're dating if we don't act like we're happy. And that requires a kiss."

Shit. How in the hell was he supposed to kiss her without becoming involved? Already he could see this was going to be much harder than he'd originally planned. Just glancing at those full ruby-red lips had him wanting to groan.

"Any more embarrassing questions?" he asked, glancing at his brothers who had all come out of their homes to see them off.

They each had their own house down the road and yet they found an excuse to be here tonight to witness them going on their first date. Though this was really not a date, but a business arrangement. He would help her, and she would keep the women off him.

"Well…" Garth his youngest brother and the one most likely to get into trouble said with a grin.

Oh no, Adrian knew Garth was going to say something that would humiliate both of them.

He pulled out several packages of condoms and handed them to Adrian. "You can never have enough of these. Here's a couple more."

A blush spread over Adrian's face and he shook his head and stuffed them into his tux pocket. There was no need for them, but he wasn't going to make a big to do in front of his brothers and embarrass Madison.

Taking her by the elbow, he led her to the door.

"On that thrilling conclusion, we're leaving. Don't wait up for us," he said which was their clue to get back to their own homes and out of his.

Holding the door open, Madison walked through and he followed her.

From outside, he could hear his brothers' laughter. Glad to have made their evening.

"Sorry about that. Garth's mouth is often a problem," he said, opening the door to his truck. He watched with fascination as she stood on the running board and then slid onto the seat. Her dress slid up exposing more of her long legs. Legs that could wrap around a man's waist.

"It's fine. He was always the troublemaking one of the group," she said. "Him and Evan."

"Nothing has changed," he said, shutting the door and walking around to the driver's side. Why did this feel like a date?

It was and it wasn't.

It was a fake date and yet Madison looked hot enough that he feared he would be the one protecting her from the single cowboys at the country club.

Once he climbed into the truck, he started it and they drove down the lane.

"We need to make a game plan," she said. "One that we're both comfortable with and that shows everyone we're a couple."

Oh, great. More about them kissing.

"Also, we need to decide when we're going to make the announcement that we're engaged. Do you have a ring or something that I can wear that would say engagement?"

Oh yes, he had the ring that he'd taken back from his ex-wife. But did he want Madison wearing that ring? It felt cursed.

"I'll get one," he said, thinking maybe he could trade it in on something that looked more like Madison. She could wear it until they broke up.

"So when will we announce we've broken up?" he asked.

"After the Cattleman's Ball. There are how many other balls or dinners before that one?"

"At least three," he said, thinking he wouldn't have to dodge over-eager young women now. And that felt really good.

"That happens the end of February, so we'll be together until then," she said. "Do you dance?"

They were not far from the country club, so they needed to make some decisions.

"Yes," he said.

"Good," she replied. "After dinner, let's dance. Hold me

really close and whisper something in my ear like you're talking about what we're going to do after we leave."

Geez, how did he do that with someone he'd always considered to be his little sister?

"Later in the evening, I want you to kiss me in front of everyone," she said. "Oh and be very attentive. Make it look like we can barely keep our hands off each other."

Shaking his head, he wondered what he'd gotten himself into. "Are you certain this is going to work?"

A smile crossed her face, "Oh yes. Just wait and see."

They pulled up in front of the country club and she looked at him and smiled. "We've got this. We can do it and you'll get what you want and I'll soon be moving to Oakdale."

The valet opened his door. "Good evening, Mr. Landry."

"Good evening," he said, stepping out and then going around to Madison's side of the truck.

Taking her hand, he helped her out and she leaned into him.

"Thank you," she said.

After taking her by the elbow, they walked into the country club where the meeting of the Texas Ranchers Association was held tonight.

Adrian gave the girl outside the restaurant their information and she led them to a table where two other couples were seated.

He pulled out her chair and she sat quite daintily for someone who could empty a mud puddle with one jump. Of course, that was twenty years ago.

"Good evening," she said, glancing around the table.

The other couples nodded and Adrian sat beside her.

"Norma Jean," he said. "I didn't know you were coming tonight."

The woman all but glared at him. "Tony asked me to be his date."

"Hello," Adrian said to the other couple while reaching across the table and shaking the man's hand. "Adrian Landry."

"Jim Burns and this is my wife, Rachel," the man said.

"My girlfriend, Madison," he said introducing her to everyone at the table.

"Norma Jean and I know each other," she said. "We went to school together."

The girl frowned. "We did."

"How are you?" Madison asked, being overly friendly.

"Fabulous," she said though the sentiment didn't reach her eyes, which had turned dark and stormy.

She was angry he'd brought someone, but frankly, he didn't care. She was the reason he and Madison were together.

Soon their food was served, and trying to remember what Madison had said about how to appear like a real couple, he lifted his fork and stared at her.

"Taste my steak," he said. Madison leaned forward, close to him, stared him in the eye, and took a bite. Her mouth wrapped around his fork.

The way she moved made it seem like they were an intimate couple, though all they'd ever done was roll around and fight in the dirt when they were children. That's when he'd learned she threw a mean right hook and given him a black eye.

She moaned. "Oh, honey, that is delicious. We should come here more often."

"We will," he said, smiling at her, and then he leaned down and kissed her on the forehead.

It was a start. A slow start, but she rewarded him with a smile.

They were faking intimacy.

"When did you two start dating?" Norma Jean asked.

Oh no, they hadn't talked about the particulars while they were in the truck.

Madison smiled. "We were childhood friends and then we saw each other again several months ago, and well, things just changed between us."

He liked how she had woven in that they had known each other a long time.

"Really?" Norma Jean said like she didn't believe them.

"Yes," he said. "Madison is so beautiful, I couldn't stop staring at her. And she's so smart. A lawyer."

Maybe that would make Norma Jean mind her manners tonight.

"What kind of law?" Norma Jean asked.

"Right now, I'm doing corporate law, but I'm opening up my own practice here in town so I can be close to my mother and Adrian," she said, gazing at him with a dark heat in her eyes.

Wow, he didn't know you could fake sexual stares, but she was doing a great job.

Dear God, did she have any idea what this did to him? Yes, they were pretending, but it felt so real, it was starting to scare him. And this was their first night. What would it be like by the time they made it to the Cattleman's Ball in February?

Norma Jean shook her head. "I'm trying to get out of this

Podunk town and back to Dallas. Why would you return here?"

Smiling at the woman, she turned to him. "To be closer to Adrian. Be prepared for a lot of traffic in the big city. If you need information about where to live, just let me know and I'll do my best to help you."

Oh, my, she was trying to help his nemesis move.

Reaching over, he put his arm around her shoulders and pulled her chair as close to his as he could.

"I like having you close by," he said quietly, intimately.

"Oh, Adrian," she said, gazing up at him. "I like being close to you as well."

While they were eating dessert, the presenter spoke about how much cattle ranching had evolved in the last year. How the price on the hoof had changed and what the outlook was for the future. Boring, typical association stuff, but it always paid to be here.

Once that was over, the band played and Madison glanced at him and smiled.

"You promised me we would dance tonight," she said.

"Let's go," he said.

They danced a slow dance and he held her snuggly against him. Close, but not indecent, and as they moved about the floor, he couldn't help but think this was nice. He liked the way they fit together.

She gazed up into his eyes like he was the only man in the building and he wondered what it would feel like to have someone act this way for real.

Leaning down, his lips covered hers as the song ended. A blast of heat from her lips went all the way to his groin, and for a second, he was shocked.

That couldn't happen. Releasing her lips, he smiled down at her.

"That was nice, but sometime tonight, you've got to give me a kiss that most women would swoon over. It's got to be a kiss that someone should say, get a room."

Dear God, could he do that? Sure it wasn't the kiss he was worried about, but rather the feelings and emotions that went along with that type of kiss. You couldn't fake a *do-me* kiss and that's what she was asking for. Or maybe you could and he just had never experienced one before.

When he walked her back to the table, Norma Jean stood. "Would you dance with me, Adrian?"

Shaking her head, Madison stared at her.

"I'm sorry," Madison said, gazing at the woman. "No one dances with my boyfriend. No one but me."

Adrian shrugged his shoulders and watched as the two women looked like they were going to come to blows over who he could dance with.

"That's not right," Norma Jean said.

"My boyfriend. My rules," Madison said smiling. "Isn't that so, Adrian?"

"Darling, whatever you want," he said, knowing she'd just blocked Norma Jean from dancing with him ever again. "Whatever makes you happy."

Norma Jean stormed away from the table and he couldn't help but lean over and whisper in Madison's ear.

"You know how to play, darling. Remind me to never go up against you in a court of law or dating."

She smiled and reached up and ran her hand down the side of his face. "Smart man. You're learning quick."

"Have to if I want to stay alive," he said grinning. "Oh no, here comes another one."

 adison had to tell three women they were not dancing with her boyfriend before the word must have spread.

She even overheard Norma Jean. "Don't even think about dancing with Adrian, not as long as that bitch is sitting beside him. She doesn't want any other woman with him."

Never before had she played the jealousy card, but tonight it felt really good to let these women know that Adrian was taken and it was hands off. So far, he was playing along really well and they had raised several eyebrows when they tangoed.

Never had she danced with someone who knew the steps to the Argentine tango. In college, she'd taken a dance class and they had worked for hours on learning the movements to the sensual dance of love.

At the end, he'd finished off with a very hot kiss and her heart pounded in her chest. No, no, no, she'd warned the poor organ.

What was she doing? This was all being done as a fake romance and yet she'd enjoyed tonight way more than any date she'd had in years. But Adrian did indeed have a flock of gold-digging women seeking him out. And Madison…

Love was not going to work for her. It was one of the reasons she'd become a lawyer. And she loved her job. Especially when she was able to work with small one-on-one clients, not big corporations who sometimes knew they were in the wrong but just wanted a lawyer to get them out of trouble. Those cases, she had to remind herself, had hired the firm she worked for and who paid her salary.

It was starting to get late and she couldn't help but think they had made progress tonight. As long as she was with him, the gold diggers had backed off.

Besides, she was starting to get tired of putting on a show for these females. After a while, it was tiring – looking happy, acting like you were in love, and staring into Adrian's eyes like she adored him.

Of course, he wasn't hard on the eyes, especially with all those firm muscles beneath his tux. And when they danced, she felt like she floated in his arms. His dark hair and light emerald eyes could send a shiver through you with just one glance.

As much as she enjoyed tonight, she had erected a wall around her heart. This gorgeous man was not going to get through that unless he used dynamite, and even then, she wasn't certain she could love again.

"Are you about ready to go?" he asked as he leaned over and whispered in her ear.

Turning toward him, she gave him her sexiest smile and leaned into his body. She wanted it to appear like they were going home to have the best sex either of them had ever experienced.

And yet they were each going home to their empty beds.

"Yes," she whispered. "But first one last dance."

A grin spread across his face, and when she stood, she noticed that Norma Jean was glaring at her like she'd like to take her outside and rumble in the parking lot.

Smiling at the woman, she and Adrian waltzed, but when the music ended, a soft, slow ballad came on that they danced up close and personal. This was the kind of dance that could get you in trouble. This was the kind of dance that made you think about things the preacher warned of. This was the kind of dance that made her think about a relationship with this man she'd known all her life.

They had been friends since they were six years old. Since the day her mother moved out of an abusive relationship and into the Landry's home to cook, clean, and watch over their children.

Adrian's mother had been expecting baby number six and they had all been hoping for a little girl. Instead, Garth arrived as vocal then as he was today.

The feel of Adrian's big, strong arms around her and her own arms around his neck warmed her body. She felt every square inch of him snug against her own, except for his manly bits. Those he had pulled back and disappointment filled her.

This was not real. And being held like this only reminded her of the many reasons why she was still single. These moments were great. Those that led to breakups were why she had decided marriage wasn't meant for her.

First, her father. Then her college boyfriend. And finally, a man she dated in law school. No, men were not for her. They were liars and cheaters who promised and never delivered.

With a sigh, she was glad she and Adrian were just friends.

Nothing more and she would need to remind herself of that on nights like tonight.

The music ended and she felt herself being leaned back in his arms and then his mouth covered hers.

The feel of his full lips covering her own, his tongue slipping in between her teeth, and the way he took control gave the ballroom audience the spectacular kiss that would have the gossips filling the local airways of how the ball had ended tonight for one couple.

When he finally ended the kiss, she lay in his arms dumbfounded. She'd been faked kissed before but nothing like this. Nothing that had heat spiraling through her straight to her center. Her lady bits clenched and sang the blues because they were going home alone.

What the hell were they doing?

"Get a room," a couple said as they walked past them.

"Thank you, we will," he replied as he lifted her to her feet and the room spun around crazily.

That kiss she'd not been prepared for. But she'd gotten the reaction she wanted.

"Let's get your coat and purse and go," he said, taking her by the hand.

"Yes," she whispered.

"Did I do all right on that final kiss?"

What in the hell was she supposed to say? Even now she was still reeling from the feel of his lips and the touch of his body against hers.

A little giggle escaped her.

"Yes," she said. "Any better and it would have to be real."

It felt odd to be critiquing his kiss, and yet, they were both trying so hard to mislead the gold diggers. Only problem was what if they entrapped themselves?

A smile crossed his face and they arrived at the table.

"Goodnight," they said.

"Wait," Norma Jean said. "Madison, we should have lunch sometime soon. Catch up and find out what's going on in each other's lives."

The woman was fishing. She wanted to try to glean information from Madison about her relationship with Adrian. Not happening.

"Oh, I'd love to Norma Jean, but until I relocate here permanently, it's going to be impossible. But I'm sure I'll see you at the next ball."

The woman frowned and nodded.

"See you next time. Adrian, call me sometime," she said. "We need to talk."

Of course, they did. She wanted to tell Adrian to dump Madison. Not happening.

"Norma Jean, we've got nothing to talk about," he said as he slipped on Madison's coat.

The woman's face turned a brilliant red and Madison feared she was going to have a stroke if they didn't leave right away.

"Goodnight," she told the woman as she placed her hand in Adrian's and they walked away.

When they were safely in the truck, she laughed. "You know what she wanted to talk to you about?"

"No," he said.

"She wants to warn you about me. Don't be taken in by a lawyer, they know how to steal all your money," she said laughing. "Also I'm sure she would tell you that you're the love of her life and she can't live without you."

A groan resounded from him. "The only one I'm not worried about is the lawyer. The rest terrify me."

She grinned in the darkened truck as they made their way back to his ranch. Tonight, she would stay with her mother. The thought of crawling into bed beside Adrian surprised her, but then again, it had been a fun evening.

And he'd been right. There were at least three women vying for his attention. At first, it had been hard to believe when he told his side, but tonight, she'd seen it firsthand. In some ways, she'd enjoyed telling each woman that her boyfriend did not dance with anyone other than her.

They had been shocked and then they grew angry before they stomped off, embarrassed. She didn't want to hurt anyone's feelings, but she was laying ground rules and doing her job to keep them at bay.

But occasionally, she thought Adrian was kind of sad he couldn't dance with the woman. What if he was truly interested in one of them?

"Are you certain you're not attracted to or interested in any of these ladies?" she asked needing to know the truth.

Quickly, his head spun in her direction. "No, I'm not. Why would you ask me that question?"

"I just wanted to make certain I didn't destroy a relationship that you later on would want to maybe create," she said.

Sighing, he shook his head. "After my divorce, I made the decision I would never remarry."

"That bad, huh?"

His eyes stayed on the road as he said, "I came home early

one day and found them in bed together. In *our* bed having sex."

Oh, that had to have hurt so badly. She'd worked a lot of infidelity divorce cases and they were the worst.

"Thank goodness you didn't have any children," she said. "That would have made it worse."

There was silence in the truck as he drove on toward the ranch.

"Did you want children?"

"Yes," he said. "Later, I learned that the reason she hadn't gotten pregnant was because she was on the pill. She *didn't* want children."

That was tough. "I'm sorry."

He shrugged. "One of the many reasons I will never marry again."

And she couldn't blame him.

They turned down the lane to the house. At the gate, it opened for him automatically.

"I know we're just friends and we're faking our relationship, but I had a fun time. Tonight felt like a success. How did it feel for you?"

He pulled up in front of the house, put the truck in park, turned off the engine, and turned to face her.

"It was the best fake date I've ever gone on," he said, his face completely serious.

She started laughing. "We could write a book. How to fake date a billionaire."

A grin spread across his face.

"You know, the only reason I'm glad that I won the lottery was it gave me the ability to keep the land. It wouldn't bring back my parents. But we saved the Kissing Oaks Ranch, and for that, I am eternally grateful."

The ranch had been in his family for over three generations and she understood why he didn't want to be the one to lose it.

After stepping out of the truck, he came around and opened her door and then helped her out.

Standing in the darkness with the moon glinting above the trees, she glanced up at him.

"I know tonight was not a real date, but I still want to tell you thank you. Thank you for the lovely evening of dancing and good food and I love the new dress."

"And the new dress loves you," he said softly. "You were the best-looking woman there."

"Thank you, now it's time I went to bed," she said. "Tomorrow I'm headed back to Dallas. In a couple of weeks, I'll be making the move here."

He took her arm and walked her across the drive and up to the front entrance.

After he opened the door, they stood inside glancing at one another awkwardly. "Have a safe trip back to Dallas."

"Thank you. And we're on again, next weekend?"

"Yes," he said. "But it's not formal. We'll be attending a barbecue. You can wear whatever you want."

She nodded. "All right. If you need me before then, just call."

"All right. I had fun tonight. Even if it was a fake date."

"Me too," she said and hurried into the kitchen toward her mother's quarters. For a moment, she was afraid he was going to kiss her again, and right now, she needed to put up more protection around her heart.

Adrian Landry's kisses were like heat-seeking missiles and she had to reinforce her defenses.

CHAPTER 5

On her mother's day off, she drove to Dallas to help Madison find a dress for the Cattleman's Ball. It was still a month away, but she wanted time to find the perfect dress and accessories.

"Why did you leave before I woke up last Sunday morning?" her mother asked.

They had already been over this, but she would tell her again. "Because I had work I needed to get finished, so I had to get back to Dallas," she said. "Besides, soon you won't be able to get rid of me."

What she wasn't telling her mother was that she wanted to leave before Adrian and his brothers asked all kinds of questions about the night before. The dancing, the kisses, and the pretending had been harder than she expected.

And those kisses of Adrian's were so damn hot. She'd needed to put space between them, so she'd left early that morning.

"Are you certain this is a good idea? The two of you pretending to date. When you were kids, I always thought that the two of you might end up together some day," her mother said.

With her arms loaded with gowns, she turned and faced her mother, surprised at her comment. "Why would you think that?"

She sighed. "I thought the two of you were always so cute together and you both seemed to gang up on the other boys. You two were the leaders and the others just followed."

Yes, but that wasn't a reason for them to become a couple. They had been close until high school. Then a girl had come between them. A girl who didn't like him being friends with Madison.

It had been years since she'd thought about that girl and she wondered where she was now. Jealous of their friendship, the girl managed to drive a wedge between them.

"You know," her mother said, "his divorce really hurt him. He couldn't wait for them to have children and then she never got pregnant," she said.

"Mom, she was taking birth control pills," Madison said. "He told me last night. And yes, the divorce hurt him badly."

Divorces were ugly. She'd dealt with them in law school, and with her own practice, she'd be dealing with them again. And then there was the story of her parents' divorce that had not been easy.

A sales clerk came to her. "Can I set you up a dressing room?"

"Yes, please," she said. Madison continued to look through the dresses on the rack. "We're friends. Nothing more."

"Yes, but friends turn into lovers and I'd hate for you to hurt him," her mother said.

Oh, that was priceless.

"What about me? What if he hurts me?"

"You've made it very clear that you never want to marry, so I'm more concerned about him. What if by doing this fake dating, he falls for you? What then?"

Why was her mother so concerned about Adrian and not her own daughter?

"We're friends. Nothing more," she said again. "Besides, I really helped him last night with his woman situation. Those bitties were after him."

But when he'd kissed her, it hadn't been nothing. It had been heat, fire, and flames, and like a plane going down, she had to come up for air.

"As my mother would say, you're playing with fire and if you're not careful one of you is going to get burned," she said, grabbing a dress off the rack and handing it to Madison. "Try this one on for me."

There was real truth to what her mother said, but she was certain she could keep her own feelings under control. She'd always liked Adrian but that didn't mean they were meant to be together.

"Mom, you can stop worrying about Adrian. I protected him from three very aggressive women who wanted to make him theirs. We laughed, we had dinner, we danced, and we played at being a real couple. It worked. And when we came home, we parted ways and I slept on your couch. I'll be back next weekend and we're attending a barbecue," she said.

Her arms were once again loaded down and she glanced toward the sales girl. "Come on, Mom, help me try these dresses on and tell me which one looks the best."

They walked into the dressing room and she shed her

jeans and shirt. She had worn shoes with a higher heel knowing she would need to know the length of the dress.

While she wiggled into the first outfit, her mother took a seat in a chair in the corner. Once she had the dress up, she turned so that her mother could zip it up.

Stepping back, she gazed at herself in the mirror. The dress was fitted and showed off her curves. She liked the color and it made her blue eyes sparkle.

"Not bad," she said, gazing at herself in the mirrors as she twirled around.

"Too tight," her mother said. "But I do like the color."

The dress was very fitted.

Turning around for her mother to unzip her, she hung up the dress on a separate hook of possibilities.

"Madison, I know you were so angry at your father for leaving us and never coming back to see you, but don't let that stop you from finding a man who loves you, getting married, and having children."

They'd had this conversation several times, too, but her mother would elaborate once more.

"Mom, like I've told you before, it's not just our family situation, though that doesn't help. I've almost walked down the aisle twice now. The first one came out as gay. And the second one cheated," she said, remembering the girl calling her up and saying she was pregnant and the father was Madison's boyfriend.

"You've had two failures. That's not the end of the world," her mother said.

"And a father who left us because his second family needed him more," she replied, recalling the hurt and anger she'd felt when she learned of his leaving.

That was when that her mother had taken the job out at the Kissing Oaks Ranch and she'd grown up there with the Landry boys. In many ways, she was stronger because of them – of the way they had not babied her but treated her like another brother.

Pulling on a soft-blue gown with a fitted bodice and layers of silk organza, her mother sighed. "That one is definitely in the keeper pile. It's gorgeous."

"But look at the skirt. It's huge. I love the color and the design, but can you see me climbing into his truck in this gown? No."

Reaching behind her, she unzipped the back partway and then let her mother do the rest.

"Maybe he would get a limo," her mother said.

"Maybe, but every time I passed a table, I'd be fighting with the skirt. I like the dress, but let's keep going." Nothing had just said *reach out and buy me*.

Grabbing the next dress off the hanger, her mother sighed. "I know little girls adore their fathers, but I always hoped you would eventually get over how your father hurt us."

She laughed. "I tried, Mother, really I did. But when he sent the invitation to his daughter's graduation when he couldn't attend mine, that incensed me. I understand he has a second family. But you don't forget about your first daughter. And who would walk me down the aisle? Him? The last time I saw him, I was sixteen and we ran into him at a store where his entire family was getting new swimsuits. Remember that? It wasn't that he planned to come see me, it was an accident with his wife gazing at us like she wanted to kill us right there in the store."

What pissed her off the most was that the man had two

children with the other woman before he decided to leave Madison and her mom to help raise the other family.

Yes, she longed for her own family, but how could she trust a man to be there for her children? Never would she ever let her son or daughter be treated like her father had forgotten them.

"Harold wasn't the smartest man," her mother said. "And he certainly couldn't keep it in his pants. She wasn't the first one he'd cheated with."

Speechless, she gazed at her mother. She'd never heard this story before. "You mean there were others?"

"Yes," she said. "I kept thinking we would leave him, and then you would meet him at the door so excited to see him. And he was so happy to see you."

"Until the day he wasn't," she said, recalling how he'd come home looking exhausted and frayed and he'd not given his usual greeting to her. What she hadn't known at the time was that he was leaving that evening for good.

As she pulled on a gold gown, her mother gazed at her. "How can my beautiful daughter not find someone who will make her a believer in love."

She gave a little laugh. "Maybe because your daughter sees too much reality that goes on between couples. I wonder if Daddy Dearest even knows I'm a lawyer. I should send him a note and offer to do his will for him."

But she wasn't that kind of lawyer, and she didn't want anything to do with her father. Not even his will.

"Madison," her mother said, "it's best if we leave him alone. Let his other children deal with him."

"True," she said.

She put on another gold gown. The skirt was not huge, but

it flowed while also clinging to her curves. It was like a dress from the movie-star era and she instantly loved it.

"That one," her mother said. "It's clingy but has those layers of soft chemise that lets you only see your curves when you walk. It's tempting and flattering and seductive all at once."

Madison nodded. "I like it. With some gold heels, it would work great."

"Maybe that dress will tempt the two of you into realizing you're perfect for one another," she said.

Laughter bubbled up from Madison. "Mom, we're not really dating. It's all a sham. And soon I'll break it off with him and we'll be done."

"But his dating problem will just start again," her mother said.

That was an issue. But Madison didn't know how to solve that problem right now. As it was, she had to pretend he was the man for her while keeping her heart from getting involved.

Love had not been kind to the women in her family, and she didn't want to make the same mistake her mother had by marrying a man who didn't know the meaning of one-man-one-woman-forever.

CHAPTER 6

Adrian glanced out at the land that had been in his family for four generations. His great-grandparents had been homesteaders who worked the land and went from living in a mud hut to a nice farmhouse with three bedrooms, an outhouse, a bathing closet, and an indoor kitchen.

Then his grandmother insisted they update the old house with indoor plumbing. It had been a great upgrade. Later, his parents added on by building two more bedrooms and a master suite for them. He missed the old house.

But with the death of their parents, the responsibility of the ranch and taking care of his brothers had fallen on him having turned eighteen a month earlier. The state had given him custody since Susan, Madison's mother, would be there helping him.

Being a teenager, he thought he knew everything, and yet he'd been dumber than a box of rocks about to be ground into dust. His lack of experience almost cost them the ranch.

The sun beat down hard on them, though the temperature

remained cool. January in Texas could be hot one minute and then an ice storm could trap you inside for days. They were predicting colder weather, so he wanted to move their herd closer to the house to get them food and water if they needed to.

His brothers sat on their horses, knowing what had to be done.

"I never heard," Blake said. "How was your date?"

Their mother had thought it would be amusing to name each of her sons the first letter of the alphabet in sequential order. But Frank had died at birth, devastating the family and leaving a hole in their hearts. Garth was the last child she'd had and was the youngest at twenty-two. None of them had married except for Adrian.

"The woman knows how to tango," he said.

Blake laughed. "You do love a woman who can dance."

"Yes, I do. You should try it sometime. It's the one place in life where a man is still in control. I lead, she follows."

Cody spoke up. "Control. You like to be in control, and women today, they don't like that."

Maybe it was true. His first wife didn't like him telling her what he thought. Was he difficult to get along with? This was why he was never going to marry again. He'd failed at ranching until he'd gotten lucky. Then he failed at marriage and filed for divorce. He wasn't willing to try again.

Cody knew women very well. Being a professional football player kept women hanging on him all the time.

"How much do I have to pay you for that advice?"

His brother shook his head. "Smart ass. I've studied women. You should try it sometime."

"Don't need to. I'm not getting married again. One and done," he said, wishing they would reach the herd so he could turn off this nonsense.

The youngest of his brothers leaned out over his horse.

"Frankly, I think Madison is smoking hot and smart. You'd be lucky to have her for a wife – a lawyer with long legs and a body that dreams are made of," Garth said.

Oh no, he didn't need his brothers thinking about Madison this way. Especially Garth, the womanizing Casanova who liked women way too much.

"Yes, that dress the other night was smoking," Evan replied. "You'd be the envy of men all over town."

Being the envy of other men didn't interest him.

"You've never told us what happened between you and Laurie. I still don't understand. And then she remarried almost immediately," Dakota said. "I really liked her."

The other brothers glared at Dakota as if saying *shut up*.

"Sometimes, Dakota, you're blind about what is going on around you. I'll explain it to you later," Blake said. "Now stop trying to ruin today. We've got a lot of work to do."

It was funny how Adrian hadn't said a word, and his brothers had come to his defense. Sometimes Dakota was too engrossed in himself and didn't see the bigger picture.

The bigger picture of running a profitable ranch and knowing how to keep them from growing broke again. Hiring the right people to teach him how to be successful and even going to college to learn about ranching.

Now his cattle were high dollar earners and his bulls were some of the most sought-after specimens. But he limited his bulls to a pasture with forty heifers. No need to wear him out.

While he was married, he'd gotten his own degree in

animal science and was using everything he'd learned to make the Kissing Oaks Ranch one of the best. And it was slowly working.

If only he'd been able to use the same techniques he'd learned in college and animal behavior on his wife. But he'd been unable to please her and she'd found refuge in another man's arms.

Today, he could think about her without hurting. But he still felt sad that he'd failed at marriage and he wasn't about to try again.

"Dakota, it doesn't matter why we divorced. She wasn't happy. Hopefully the man she married can make her happy," he said softly.

They rode along in silence. A cold blustery wind blew and he pulled his coat tighter.

"Dad had a hard time making Mother happy some days," Blake said. "I'm beginning to wonder if we're meant to marry. What if we can't find anyone who pleases us? Not many women like living out on a ranch in the middle of nowhere. They think because we now have money, we should be jetting around somewhere. But there is nothing like the peaceful sound of silence out in the fields."

They all murmured their agreement. It was true. It only took Adrian a couple of days in the big city before he was ready to return to the ranch where it was quiet.

"I will say that you and Madison made a mighty nice-looking couple," Cody said. "And she grew up around here. It's why she wants to return. I think you should seriously consider her."

That wasn't going to happen. All he wanted was for her to be his fake date for the rodeo season. Once that was over, then they would part ways and she would have her law practice and he would go back to working the ranch business.

Somehow he had to get his brothers' attention off Madison.

"But what if they broke up?" Evan cut in. "Then Susan would be upset, and she might quit. Who would cook our dinner, do our laundry, and make those great cookies she bakes? Sorry, but I'm not willing to lose Susan over Madison."

Even though mischievous, Evan was always the practical one. And food was very important to him.

"Madison will be my escort until after the rodeo season and then we'll separate as friends. She's doing me a favor and I'm doing her one as well. It's a business arrangement, nothing more. So don't be worried about us breaking up or losing her mother as our savior."

"I ate enough crap while in college. She cooks good meals," Evan said, proving Adrian's point.

A chuckle came from Garth. "I think Cody is right. It's time you found yourself another wife and Madison is perfect. Take a chance. I'm going to bet you a new colt that by the end of the ball season you'll be dating seriously. Anyone want to take me up on my bet?"

Certainly, they would not be dating. He could win this bet.

"I'll take you up on it," Adrian said. He really would like one of Dakota's colts from his stallion. The horse was magnificent. "I'll bet you a trip to Vegas that we're not dating by the end of the last ball."

"You're on," Dakota said. "As long as it's during championship week."

"That's not until December," Adrian said.

"So, I can wait. Because I'm going to win this challenge," he said.

"What makes you say that?" Adrian asked, wanting to know what to look out for.

The man laughed. "I'm not telling you, but I think the two of you are perfect for one another. Sometimes the universe delivers what you need. Just like that lucky Powerball ticket. We needed a break and we received one. You need a good woman and I think the universe just delivered."

"That's bullshit," Cody replied. "Total bullshit, nonsense."

Dakota shrugged. "Think what you want, but I believe Madison is the perfect woman for Adrian."

This was making him uneasy. Maybe he should cancel their next date. He'd had fun at the country club event, but he wasn't looking for anything serious.

"Are you certain she's not after your money like the others?" Cody asked. "Maybe she's just smarter about the way she's going about this."

It was terrible how they all now questioned whether someone was just being their friend because they had money.

"She's a lawyer," Blake said. "She's probably making a million a year on her own."

They rode over the top of the hill and there were their cattle grazing down below. It was time to put an end to this nonsense and get to work. The herd was all together until roundup in the spring. But until this cold weather pattern passed, they needed to be closer.

"Damn, we're lucky men," Garth said, gazing out at the rolling pastures. "Our great-grandparents did us well."

"Yes, until that damn twister struck," Evan said. Their parents' deaths had been hard on all of them, but Evan took it the hardest. He'd been extremely close to their mother and finding her body beneath the house ruins had been tough.

Since then, Adrian had made a rule that every house built on their property had a storm shelter. The house might be destroyed, but if they were down in the storm shelter, they hopefully would survive.

"When is the Cattleman's Ball?" Dakota asked, obviously still thinking about the bet they just made instead of the job at hand.

"Not until the end of February. Hopefully all this cold weather will be done by then," Adrian said.

The ball was held each year in Fort Worth. And while Adrian could get hotel rooms for them both, he really didn't like spending the night there. He'd just drive his truck into Fort Worth and then come home. He'd need to check with Madison. By the end of February, she might be living in Oakdale.

"Let's get started," he said. "We've got almost a thousand head of cattle to move."

"I agree. I've got to work when I get home," Dakota said.

"You writing a new novel?"

"Yes, I am," he said. "And no there are no cowboys or cattle in my book."

"Damn shame," Blake told him. "I'd read it if there were."

"It's a romance," he said. "Women love them."

Adrian laughed so hard, he nearly fell off his horse. It was hard to believe that his brother was a best-selling romance author. But then, if it brought his brother happiness, he shouldn't care.

"Let's go," Cody said and they split up, going different directions and surrounding the herd.

The image of Madison flashed in his brain. All those damn curves in that dress. And her kiss. What he wouldn't tell his brothers was how that kiss had left him wanting more. A lot more.

And he'd made that stupid bet just to make certain he didn't succumb to the desire he felt after one of her kisses.

CHAPTER 7

*S*aturday had come and Madison drove out to see her mother. Plus, she and Adrian needed to go into town. If people were going to believe in their engagement, they had to be seen together.

Today, she'd worn a sweater since the air had become cold. Last night, a front came through, and while it wasn't bad, today the highs were only in the fifties, and with the wind chill, the air felt like it was below freezing.

Sitting in the kitchen, her mother gazed at her. "Do you really think this phony engagement to Adrian is a good idea?"

After the night at the country club, she had questioned her decision. She'd never pretend to kiss someone before, and that one had been the most uncontrollable kiss she'd experienced in years.

Not since her breakup with her ex-fiancé. And even then, she didn't remember his kisses being that explosive. Maybe it was just her. Maybe Adrian was a good kisser and she'd been alone for so long that her body lit up at the feel of his lips.

"Mom, I need his help to support my law practice here. If I don't receive his help, then I probably couldn't move. And I so want to be closer to you and to get out of the big crowds and traffic. I've had enough corporate law to last me a lifetime," she said, thinking how her firm had not been happy when she announced she was leaving. She was not even near making partner. But she was a workhorse in their firm because she was single and had plenty of time on her hands. Well, now, her time would be spent working on her own clients. Not theirs.

The smell of cake permeated the air and she knew her mother was making the boys, the Landry men, yellow cake with chocolate frosting.

Adrian walked into the room, and she had to stop herself from staring. His jeans fit his well-muscled thighs and he wore a pressed shirt in soft green that made his emerald eyes pop. In his hands, he carried a black hat.

"Hey," he said. "I've been looking for you."

"Oh," she said. "What's up."

"Instead of us going to the country club or a restaurant tonight, would you like to go with me to the Burnett Ranch? It's about an hour from here. I need to look at a couple of horses and talk to Travis about buying some of his heifers this spring."

Madison had been friends with Desiree Burnett for many years. They had met during a rodeo when they were both barrel racers. It'd been a long time since she'd seen her friend and her response was automatic.

"Yes, let's go," she said. "Am I dressed all right?"

His eyes skimmed down her sweater, jeans, and boots.

"You look perfect to me," he said.

She turned to her mom. "Bye, Mom. I'll talk to you later tonight."

"Be careful," she said.

"I thought maybe we could stop at a restaurant between here and there and grab a bite to eat," he told her, taking her elbow and leading her outside where his truck was parked.

"Sounds good to me," she said.

After he helped her into the truck, she realized he had a top-of-the-line vehicle. But then again, why wouldn't he? He'd won the freaking lotto, and she didn't know if that was a help or a hindrance.

Once he was inside, he started the truck up, and they traveled down the road.

"How was your week?" he asked.

"I gave my notice at the firm and they aren't thrilled I'm leaving. Even offered me a pay raise, but I said no. I want out of there. Is it wrong to want a slower lifestyle with time for me and with my mom?"

"No," he said, glancing at her. "You never know when a tornado is going to completely destroy your life."

With a sigh, she felt like a heel. She'd forgotten that was how his parents were taken. That day in high school, she would never forget. It had gotten so dark, and then the winds came. She remembered huddling inside the hall with the other students, her hands over her head, kneeling in front of the lockers. Like that would do a lot of good if a funnel of wind swirling three hundred miles an hour hit the school building.

"That day was a living nightmare. Do you remember the sirens blaring and the winds howling?" she asked.

"Yes," he said. "All I could think about was that Dad had

promised Mom for twenty years that he was going to build a storm shelter. And he never did."

Madison remembered when they finally let school out, Adrian and his brothers rushed home and discovered the destruction of their home and their parents buried beneath the rubble holding one another. Nothing was ever the same on the ranch after that.

A gust hit the side of the truck and she noticed how he gripped the wheel. "The wind is really fierce today."

"Yes," he said.

"Often," Madison said softly, "I think that if my mother had not been at the grocery store that day, she would have been in the house with your parents."

"Yes," he said with a slight squeak in his voice before clearing his throat. "Now any home built on the Kissing Oaks Ranch must have a storm shelter built inside. Either a room or a cellar beneath the house. If I can help it, we will never lose another family member to a tornado."

They rode in silence for a few minutes and she enjoyed the scenery along the highway.

"Tell me about winning the lottery. Were you surprised?"

A smile crossed his face. "After Mom and Dad's deaths, you left for college and I'd been in charge of the ranch. Of course, I didn't have a clue as to what I was doing. We were close to losing the land. I bought the ticket on a whim. I never thought we would win, but I was kind of desperate."

She'd never heard that he was about to lose the ranch. That was surprising. And to think that money he won saved his inheritance.

"It wasn't until the next day that I heard the winning ticket had been sold there in town at the Beer and Bait shop, which was where I purchased the ticket. I found the ticket and then I sat there stunned."

Reaching across the seat, she squeezed his arm. "I'm so happy you won, especially since you were about to lose your home."

The ranch had been ingrained into his soul and she knew he would've been devastated if he'd lost the family home.

"What was the first fun thing you did?"

"I took my brothers on a trip to the Bahamas where I laid some ground rules. This was *my* money, but I wanted to share it with them. But in order to receive their trust fund, they had to finish college. Only Blake fought me. The rest were good. This way, they received an education in case something happened to the ranch or we lost the money. They need to know how to take care of themselves."

After a pause, he asked, "Whatever happened to that gaggle of girls you called half sisters?"

She laughed. The "wicked witches" was a more appropriate title. But being they were truly her half sisters, she couldn't say that out loud.

"Mother took my father aside and told him that if they mistreated me again, he would never get to see me." She sighed. Families could be difficult and it was one of the reasons why she never intended to marry or have children. She didn't want anyone else to suffer what she'd been through. "I never saw him again."

Adrian's head swiveled toward her. "You're kidding me."

"Nope. Not a birthday, Christmas card, or graduation event did my father attend. I guess the wicked half sisters were more important," she said.

Even today it hurt to think of how he'd chosen them over

her, and how he'd laughed when her mother told him how the sisters had treated Madison when she went to visit him. He didn't love his own daughter.

"Damn," Adrian said.

"Yes, damn," she agreed. "With a childhood like mine, how can you have your own family? My biggest fear is getting married, having a child, and then divorcing."

The truck hit a bump in the road and they bounced.

"I'm thankful that me and Laurie never had children. We were trying or at least I thought we were until I found the birth control pills in her purse. That was when I began to suspect that all was not well in paradise."

Glancing at him, she could see the pain on his face. "You really loved her?"

He sighed. "No, I married her because it was what she wanted. She had some dream of me not working, us flying around the world, buying a yacht. That's not me. It's not the life I want. All I wanted was to make certain the ranch became a success and have a family with all of us spending time together. Our dreams didn't match, and she went in search of her dream."

She laughed. "Sorry, but I can't see you on a yacht. A big, strong cowboy like yourself. Did she have her eyes open when she married you?"

Laughter filled the truck.

"Money does things to people," he said. "I can't tell you how many people showed up at the ranch wanting money. Family members I'd never heard of. At first, I gave in to the hard luck stories, and then when I hired a money manager, he said it all stopped now. He said have charities contact me and then we can sit down once a month and decide who to donate money to. He also is the one who insisted that I hire security for the ranch. A wise man."

The thought of winning billions was not something she could even comprehend.

"And now you have me to be your pretend fiancée," she said with a laugh. "And I'm a good choice. A woman who doesn't want to be married, who is not interested in your money, but only being your attorney."

A grin spread across his face. "So when is the fake engagement announcement."

"At the next ball, you will make a grand gesture in front of everyone," she said with a laugh. "A photographer will take our picture and put it in the newspaper. I've got to find just the right dress."

"Do you need more money?"

"No, Adrian, you've given me enough," she said. "I'll be collecting enough from you in billable hours."

He turned down the road that led to the Burnett's ranch and getaway.

"I've known you since you were a little girl," he said. "Who would have ever thought that we would be two lonely people both determined to never marry again."

"So true," she said.

They pulled up to the gate and he gave the attendant his name.

"Yes, sir, I see your name right here. They are expecting you down at the barn," he said.

"Thanks," Adrian replied as the gate opened and he went through onto the Burnett ranch.

Driving slowly, he went past the reception center and the cabins and then he pulled into a parking place by the barn.

"I shouldn't be too long," he said.

"No worries. I'm going to go find Desiree and catch up with her."

After he climbed out of the truck, he came around and helped her out. Then he leaned down and kissed her on the forehead. "Have fun."

"Thanks," she said as she watched him stroll into the barn. During the years since high school, he'd become a muscular man with strong legs and arms that showed he lifted weights. But what she really liked was the way his hair lay against his forehead with just a swatch peeking out from beneath his hat. And those emerald eyes. Dark and gleaming that left you feeling breathless.

They were doing little affectionate things to make people believe they were dating, but there was no one around and yet he'd kissed her on the forehead. Strangely, she wanted more and knew that was not possible.

"Madison," she heard her friend squeal and she turned to her.

They met in the middle of the parking lot and hugged.

"How are you?" Desiree asked.

"Good," she said with a grin as she hooked her arm through hers. "Let's go catch up. It's been so long since I've seen you."

"Yes," Desiree said. "Come on, I want to show you something."

Madison was shocked when they went into cabin five. There Desiree had tea and blueberry trifles set up.

"How nice," Madison said.

"Oh, just wait," Desiree said. "Remember how I told you

that my great-great-great-great-grandmother had visited me?"

"Yes," Madison replied, taking a bite of the trifle. It was so good.

"You really didn't believe me, did you?" Desiree said.

What could Madison say? It was hard to believe that her friend had seen an actual ghost.

"I'm hoping she'll join us today for tea," she said laughing.

What? A ghost? Really?

"Okay," Madison said, wondering if her friend needed counseling of some sort.

"You see, she's been matchmaking all my cousins. So far, she's found a wife for Travis, Tanner, Tucker, Joshua, and Jacob. As the original owner of the ranch, she's determined that the Burnett line will continue." Desiree giggled. "As long as she leaves me alone, I'm fine."

Madison didn't know what to say. She'd never really given ghosts much thought.

"What about you? Have you found anyone since your last breakup?"

Why did everyone think that you had to find love or you weren't happy?

"No and yes," she said, thinking of the impending fake engagement. "All I can say is that I will never marry. After going through my parents' divorce and then after my engagement ended, I'm just not interested in finding a man."

Desiree frowned. "But what about a family?"

"No kids," she said.

Still, the chances of divorce were just too high. She wasn't willing to risk going through what her mother had. Or her children being disappointed with their parents.

For a moment, Desiree sat quietly.

"I'm not willing to risk my child being treated like I was by my father and my half sisters."

Taking a deep breath, Desiree stared at her. "Someday you may change your mind and that's all right. Travis said he would never marry again and here he is married with a little boy and another baby on the way. He's happy."

Madison remembered how Travis's wife and their unborn child had been killed in a tragic accident that involved a drunk. It had been such a sad time and even Madison had attended the funeral to support the Burnett family.

Just then the smell of lavender filled the air.

"Where is that coming from?"

"It's my grandmother," Desiree said. "I want you to meet Eugenia Burnett. She's been matchmaking our family for generations."

Just then an apparition slowly came into view. The image of a grandmother wearing a long blue dress, her white hair up in a bun, appeared.

"Nice to meet you, Madison," she said.

Madison stared, gobsmacked, at what she was seeing. Was she real?

"Dear, I heard what you said about not getting married and having children. I'm so, so sorry you feel that way. I saw you come in with such a nice-looking young man," she said sinking down into a rocking chair in the corner.

Desiree laughed as the elder gazed at Madison. "From your expression, I can see that you're shocked."

"Of course, I am," Madison said. "I'm a lawyer. I'm trained to look at things in an observant manner. How are you projecting her?"

"I'm not," she said.

"If only I could have a bite of that trifle," she said, her wrinkled hand reaching out. She sighed. "But I can't eat."

"Are you dating Adrian?" Desiree asked her. "I know you rode over here with him but are the two of you seeing each other."

All Madison could do was stare at the older woman rocking there in the chair. "Yes and no. I'm helping him out by attending some balls this season with him. He's helping me out by being my first big client in my new law practice."

"You're opening your own practice?"

"Yes," she said. "Back in Oakdale. After my mother's stroke, I decided it was time to move closer to her."

Desiree's face lit up with happiness. It would be great to be close to her friend again.

"Oh my goodness, we'll be so close," Desiree said. "I'm so excited."

The ghost nodded and smiled. "Adrian. I like that name. You two look very good together and I think there is something between the two of you. I'm going to make a prediction that you'll eventually marry him." She sighed. "If you both stayed here, I could make certain the two of you came together."

What? No. That couldn't happen.

The ghost could predict all she wanted, but there would be no wedding between her and Adrian. And yet, there was the bogus engagement coming up and she couldn't tell her friend because then the truth might get out.

"No," she said.

The ghost laughed. "You're as bad as my grandsons. None of those kids thought they would marry and now more than almost half of them are happily hitched. When the time is right, Desiree will wed, but now is not the right time. I haven't found her the perfect husband, but I will. And you, dear. You must learn to forgive so that you can marry that handsome cowboy who is buying a horse from Travis."

Madison was not going to argue with a ghost. It would just be a waste of good breath. The apparition could believe what she wanted, but she wouldn't be marrying Adrian.

"It's been a pleasure meeting you. But I must get back to working on Justin," she sighed. "That boy is impossible."

Standing, she blew a kiss toward Desiree. "Madison, believe child. Believe that you are worthy of a good man. A man who will adore you. Forgive and be healed."

And just like that, there were sparkles in the room as she left.

Why should she be the one to forgive? Her father was the one who walked away from her. Walked away and never looked back.

"Isn't she something else?" Desiree said smiling. "I'm sorry if she upset you."

"Oh no, she didn't upset me. But I'm not getting married or having children. And my father is not worth my time. Forgiveness is not necessary when you no longer care."

CHAPTER 8

As they left the Burnett's, he noticed that Madison was quiet. Normally, she was much more outgoing, but after her visit with Desiree, she seemed more introspective.

"Did you enjoy visiting with Desiree?"

She laughed. "Yes, I did."

He was glad to hear her laughter. The sound soothed him and filled him with warmth. Yes, they were a pretend couple, but he would always want her to be happy.

"Did you know they have a ghost?"

That was an odd statement.

"I saw her," she said. "She's been matchmaking Desiree's cousins. Seems she's been on the Burnett ranch for years."

That was strange, but then again, a bunch of the Burnetts had married over the last couple years. Five of them to be exact. And poor Travis had sworn he would never remarry after the loss of his wife and baby.

"What's her name?"

"Eugenia Burnett. She is one of the original founders of the Burnetts and she's determined that the ranch continue."

He laughed. "Well, I don't think they have to worry."

Shaking her head, she sighed. "I can't help thinking about what she said to me. Told me I needed to forgive. I'm supposed to just let go and forgive my father." Shaking her head, she laughed. "That's not going to happen."

Madison had every right to hate her father like she did, but he also knew from experience that it was better to just let go and forgive someone. That way you weren't filled with hate and anger. Just like he'd had to forgive Laurie.

And that had been tough.

Still, that didn't mean he wanted to remarry.

"A ghost. Sounds like a really good marketing idea. Tell people if they come to your cabins, you'll be on a working ranch with a matchmaking ghost who will also find you your perfect mate," he said with a flourish.

They both laughed and she sighed.

"I didn't think it was real, either, but Desiree assured me Eugenia was not some machine that showed her picture on the wall. And she did respond to me."

Maybe to the Burnetts, she was real, but not to Adrian. Why wouldn't his parents have returned to guide him and give him directions when he needed them the most if there were ghosts?

"And the smell when she arrived," she said almost to herself.

"If she's been dead awhile, she must have stunk," he said.

"No, she smelled like lavender," she replied surprised.

"A ghost," he said, twirling the thoughts in his head.

"A matchmaking ghost. So far five of the Burnetts have

married because of her," she said shaking her head. "She said you were a handsome cowboy."

He grinned. "And she wanted to find me a wife?"

"Oh yes," she said. "Me. I told her that was not happening."

"I'd be a damn good catch," he said grinning.

"We both understand what we're doing here," she said. "Only thing happening between us is fake dating with a fake engagement."

For a moment, they were silent as they traveled down the road. It felt comfortable being with Madison. And if they hadn't both been burned by life, there might have been something between them. So far, they were having fun, and there wasn't an expectation between them.

And so far, kissing her had been enjoyable. As in way too much fun. When he had helped her out of the truck at the Burnetts, it just seemed natural to pull her in close and kiss her. At the last moment, he'd diverted his mouth from her lips to her forehead.

As they got near the edge of town, he glanced at her. "Are you hungry?"

"Yes," she said.

"Want to go to the busiest restaurant in town on Saturday night?"

She grinned. "I'd love to. It's been years since I ate there."

As they reached the edge of the city limits, he pulled into a restaurant on the big lake. Catfish Cafe. It looked more like a dive, but the food was excellent.

After he parked the truck, he came around and helped her out. Taking her by the arm, they walked into the packed restaurant. Mostly it was filled with locals and he immediately recognized several ranchers and their families.

"If you wanted us to be seen together, this is the place to be," he said, whispering low into her ear.

She smiled up at him and his heart skipped a beat. Making her happy filled him with joy.

"Good," she said. "That way it won't be a surprise when we announce our engagement."

A chuckle rumbled through his chest. And yet, part of his mind was screaming warning sirens. He liked being with Madison. He liked the way they were as a couple and there was no pressure with her.

Their waitress took them to a table in the center of the room. Not far from them was Sally Jones–the lady who was always flashing him her long legs and grinning at him. Sometimes he feared she was going to pull a naughty stunt and spread her legs and he would have to quickly turn away.

A smile filled her face until he pulled out Madison's chair and seated her. Then her eyes narrowed and he feared that if there was a knife at Sally's table, Madison could be in trouble.

He nodded his head toward Sally and leaned in close to Madison. "Second most ardent admirer is at a table at ten o'clock."

She leaned up and ran her hand down his face. "Good to know."

After he was seated, she put her hands on the table and he took her hand in his. "We're getting really good at this."

Suddenly her bare foot was running up his leg. His dick swelled at the feel of her foot caressing his muscle. Damn, pretending was even hard when she did things like this.

"She's watching, so I'm giving her a show," she said grinning.

He could see that the little minx was enjoying what she

was doing to him. And sadly, he liked the feel of her foot through his jeans.

"Darling," he said leaning in close. "I could get used to this."

She giggled just as the waitress came to take their order.

While they waited for their food, they held hands and leaned across the table to talk to one another.

"We could be in a movie," she said. "We're acting and doing a really good job."

Only problem was that he was having to remind his dick this was not for real. This was for show. Only. There would be no driving her home later and taking her to bed.

Where had that thought come from?

And she was probably staying with her mother tonight in his home.

"Do you think we could win an Oscar for our performance?" he asked, trying to keep this lighthearted and fun while his breath seemed to die in his throat. Tiny tremors of heat zinged through him and his jeans had grown tight in the groin area.

This was all play. Just like the feelings he was experiencing right now. They had to be fake, because if they were real, he would be in so much trouble.

"Oh no, Norma Jean just joined Sally for dinner," she said smiling. She released his hand and waved.

"We do know how to draw a crowd," he said, leaning toward her and kissing her briefly on the lips as he knew they were all staring at them.

She giggled and he loved that sound. It was carefree and fun.

The waitress brought their dinners. "Enjoy," she said.

They separated and gazed down at the food on their plate.

Why was he suddenly not hungry? The only thing he wanted was to feel Madison's hand in his again.

"Oh, this looks so good," she said as she dug into the catfish.

It was perfection. The food was delicious, the company was outstanding, and right now, he was miserable in his tight jeans. Why did it feel like tonight something had changed between them? Or was it there all along, and he'd just ignored the way she made him laugh and the ease of their relationship?

With a sigh, he finished his food and leaned back. If they were married, he would take her home and carry her up the stairs to his bed. There he would unwrap her like a gift and explore every inch of her satiny skin. Taste her in every area and have her crying out his name as he took her.

But he was just fantasizing.

"Oh my goodness, that was so good," she said. "I'm stuffed."

It was time to take her back to her mother. Back to his house and let her go, because if he held onto her, then he would lose her.

"Are you ready?" he asked.

"Yes," she said softly.

After he paid the bill, they stood. The other table was also leaving at the same time. Damn, his timing really sucked.

Putting his hand on Madison's back, he guided her out the door.

"Adrian," Sally called.

Crap, they were not going to escape without talking to the two women he avoided at all costs.

They stepped outside the restaurant into the cool evening

air and the women followed. There was no evading these two man-traps.

"Adrian," Norma Jean called.

Slowly, he turned and stared into her cold gray eyes. In some ways, she reminded him of Laurie, but with a lot more need for control. "Hi, ladies. Did you enjoy the food?"

"Very much," Sally said.

They had not said hello to Madison. Bitches.

"You ladies, know my date, Madison," he asked to draw their attention to the fact that he was with a woman.

"Hi," they each responded in a deadpan.

"Yes, we know each other," Norma Jean said. "Your date? I thought you didn't date."

Caught in a second lie.

"Only occasionally," he said. "We've just hit it off so well, we're seeing each other daily."

They would think he was sleeping with Madison, but he didn't care. People were going to think what they wanted.

"Oh," Sally said. "But you're not engaged. You're not exclusive, right?"

Still looking for an opening. A way to get to him.

Suddenly Madison reached up, her hand cupping his cheek, she pulled his mouth toward hers and he met her halfway.

The kiss was deep and passionate and filled with the promise of more. The promise of love and sex and all the things they were avoiding. And yet, he couldn't resist pulling her close and holding her tight.

The feel of her breasts crushed against his chest almost had him moaning. There was so much more he wanted from Madison, but this was only for these two ladies to witness.

Madison was going to give them a show and he was her lead actor. Whatever she wanted, he would have given it to her at this moment. This kiss had his erection squeezing his jeans tight.

The feel of her in his arms was more thrilling than he'd planned. What in the hell was he doing? If they were doing this to be a show, it was starting to have real consequences for him.

When she broke loose, he pushed back her hair that had fallen in her face and she smiled at the two ladies.

"We're exclusive. He's mine," she said. "It was great seeing you two."

They stared at them, their mouths hanging open.

As they walked off, a chuckle rumbled through him. "Damn, that was perfect, honey. I enjoyed every minute of it."

She probably thought he was talking about the show they had just put on, but in reality, it was her kiss. The feel of her lips had left his heart pounding in his chest with his dick throbbing in time.

Whatever was happening between them, he liked it and now he just wondered if he'd made a terrible mistake hiring her as his bodyguard.

What had she just done?

As Adrian helped her up in the truck and closed the door, she took a deep breath and tried to compose herself. Her legs had felt like spaghetti noodles walking to the vehicle.

Where had she gotten the courage to kiss him like that in front of those two witches?

In fact, she had wanted to continue kissing him right there. It was like she'd gone into a world without anything but Adrian. Like everything around her disappeared at the touch of his lips on hers.

Once their lips fused, he'd taken control, and all she'd wanted to do was surrender to the feelings he evoked. And that was not a good reaction for a pseudo-relationship.

Even now her center throbbed with heat she could not remember ever feeling. What was she doing?

Opening the driver's door, he stepped inside the truck shaking his head.

"Remind me to never get into an argument with you or do

any kind of side deals. You could probably outwit Einstein," he said laughing. "Did you see their faces?"

She had and enjoyed every moment of them realizing their defeat. But what would the future bring? Sure, they could make everyone believe they were a couple, but what happened when they broke up?

"Yes, especially Norma Jean's expression," she said. "Honestly, I hope she finds a man and settles down and lives a great life."

The woman was catty and insensitive, but still, Madison didn't want to wish ill will on her. Everyone deserved happiness.

"Just not with me," he said. "And, Sally, I feel sorry for her. But that doesn't mean I want to spend the rest of my life with her either. And I feared they were going to gang up on me and somehow trap me into marriage."

She'd seen cases where women did this to rich men. But Adrian seemed like a man who had a good head, and she doubted that anyone could ever convince him to marry again.

The man had a sweet heart and didn't want to hurt these women, but he was tired of them pursuing him.

With a sigh, she leaned back against the truck's seat. The kiss had happened spontaneously without her giving much thought to it. All she'd wanted to do was brand him as hers before the women were emboldened to do something to Adrian. That kiss had let everyone know that he was hers. Back off.

And yet, it also frightened her. She couldn't do that again. Especially after the reaction she'd experienced to his lips.

More and more, she enjoyed spending time with Adrian. More and more, she felt a hot rush of heat fill her center, making her legs go limp, her body wanting to cling to his when their lips touched. More and more, she could feel herself developing feelings that were unwanted by both of them.

"Thank you for pointing out that I was there. Those women didn't want to acknowledge me. The housekeeper's daughter," she said.

A frown appeared on his face that she could see in the light from the dashboard.

"Why wouldn't they want anything to do with the housekeeper's daughter?"

She laughed. "You obviously don't know how mean girls can be in high school. Yes, we're not in school any longer, but they can still be mean bitches."

For a moment, he was silent. "Madison, you're smart. You've got a great career and you're beautiful. Why do you think they want a husband?"

She shrugged. "To make beautiful little babies they can entrap men with?"

"Exactly. Those ladies are looking for someone to take care of them. They don't want to work or have a job. All they want is for some man to put them in a life of ease. Can you imagine what those women would have been like in the old days when our grandparents worked so hard to make a living off the ranch?"

"No," she said. "In some ways, I feel sorry for them too. Being self-sufficient is a wonderful thing. No matter what happens, I can always take care of myself. Even if my practice fails, I will go back to work for a group of lawyers."

"Your practice is not going to fail," he said with the confidence she didn't feel.

Hope filled her and she prayed he was right. "At ten clients, I break even."

"See, you've already done the numbers and know what it's going to take to be successful."

He turned down the ranch road to the house. When they came close, the gate opened automatically. As they bounced down the lane, she wasn't ready for the night to end. Suddenly he pulled the truck over about a half mile from the gate.

"Why did you stop?"

A grin spread across his face and he leaped out of the truck and ran around to her side and helped her out.

"Don't worry, the rattlesnakes are hibernating. We should be safe," he said.

"What are you doing?"

"Look up?" he said, wrapping his arm around her shoulder and pulling her in close. "Look at that moon. It's so full and bright. It's beautiful. You don't get that kind of moon in Dallas."

It was true, and yet all she could think about was the way his arm felt around her and the closeness of his body. It was like she'd come home and this was where she belonged. The aroma of a strong man overwhelmed her and she liked the smell.

A cow mooed in the distance as they stood there, arm in arm, gazing up at the moon. The bright light reflected off the pasture. The night echoed with the sound of a coyote bemoaning his loneliness.

"He's calling for his mate," Adrian said as they leaned against the truck.

If they were actually dating, she would have loved that they had stopped somewhere along the road and were out gazing at the land and the moon and the cattle. But instead, all she could think about was that kiss and now she wanted him to kiss her again. To once again feel his lips caressing hers.

So far, she felt like she'd been instigating most of the kisses, except for that very sweet, gentle kiss he'd given her earlier on the Burnett's property. And that one had been so good.

But this relationship was not going anywhere. It was doomed to fail before it began. And yet, she had not experienced these emotions since Randall, her former fiancé. Looking back, they had not been right for one another. She didn't even fully understand why she'd accepted his proposal. But it had finalized her feelings on marriage.

"Why did your family name this the Kissing Oaks Ranch?"

Maybe her mother had told her when she was a kid, but she didn't remember, and now she wanted to know.

"You see that old, gnarled oak tree in the distance?"

"Yes," she said, squinting at the tree in the shadow of the moonlight.

"My great-grandparents, the original settlers, were married beneath that tree. There is a superstition in our family that your marriage will last if you ask the person you love to marry you beneath that tree."

Strange how families developed superstitions or ghosts or other things to keep them together. Maybe it was why her parents' marriage didn't last, because they had no traditions, no superstitions. And they most certainly had not liked one another.

"Did you ask Laurie to marry you beneath that tree?" she asked.

He was silent and then with a sigh he replied, "No. She wouldn't go horseback riding with me. And she was definitely not going to walk across a field filled with cow patties and possibly rattlesnakes to see an old tree. She didn't know until later the significance of that tree in our family. By then, it didn't really matter. She laughed at the very idea of such nonsense."

They watched the moon's shadow dance over the grass, both of them silent.

"Your family has such a rich, colorful history," she said. "The Burnetts have a wonderful history too. My parents didn't have any of that and now the only thing we share is a divorce. You're so lucky to have this story to tell your children."

It was another reason not to have children. What could she tell them about their lineage? Oh, your grandparents hated each other so much that your grandfather created a second family and when your grandmother found out, he left. Then he dumped his daughter for them.

"I feel very blessed to have been raised by loving parents and grandparents and the times we have on this land. And you can't imagine the horror I had of almost losing this place when I was eighteen. It would have devastated me. Honestly, I think my great-grandparents probably helped me win that lottery. That's why it's so important to me, that I make this place a success. I've been given a second chance. I doubt there would be a third."

A shiver of cold went through her. It was the first of February and they were out gazing at the moon in the darkness. And yet, she was enjoying every minute of being with Adrian.

"And now you have something that your children will tell their children about," she said.

"I hope so. Are you cold?"

"A little, but I'm enjoying being out in the country at night, listening to the cows, watching the moon, and just talking to someone I enjoy being with."

Had she said too much? It was true. She liked Adrian. Always had, ever since her mother came to work at the ranch. He'd been her favorite Landry boy.

Pulling her in front of him, he wrapped his arms around her to keep her warm.

"This is peaceful, isn't it?"

"Yes," she said. "In Dallas, I would be listening to sirens and cars and airplanes. Occasionally, a gunshot. But here, all I hear are cattle and the gentle breeze blowing through the grass."

"Don't forget the coyotes," he said.

She laughed. "Can't forget the coyotes."

She liked the feel of his body snug against her own and the heat that flowed from him to her as they stared out at the pasture.

"Look, a shooting star," she cried suddenly. "We need to make a wish."

"A wish?" he said.

"Yes, haven't you heard that you should wish upon a shooting star?"

"No, I was told that meant someone died," he said.

"I like my version better," she told him as she closed her eyes and wished.

It was a strange wish, a mixture of wanting and longing. A wish that she was willing to try marriage and have children, but only if she could do it with this man. Eugenia, the ghost, had told her they would marry, but Madison didn't believe in ghosts or their matchmaking abilities.

Right now, it was a magical night and she needed to keep her mind and heart focused on what this time was all about. Helping Adrian with his women problem and setting up her practice in town.

He didn't believe in marriage and neither did she. But there was a rapidly forming bond between them. A bond that felt good. A bond that had her imagining things she had no business thinking about.

"What did you wish for?"

"If I told you, then it wouldn't happen," she said but then grinned. "I wished that my dreams would come true. That soon I'll be living here in town and practicing law, making enough money to live comfortably."

His arms squeezed her and a delicious spiral of passion made its way through her body.

"You don't want to live rich? Drive a fancy sports car, own a yacht, and fly somewhere new each weekend?"

"Not really," she said. "I own a jeep that I love. Flying has become a hassle, though I do love a nice vacation once a year. But every weekend? No. A yacht? What would I do with that?"

He laughed.

"More than anything, I like the freedom of owning my own practice. Making my own hours, being able to take off when I need to, and I don't want to screw people out of money. I just want enough to live comfortably."

It was true. Sure, if she had a nice big fat bank account, it would be reassuring that she would never go hungry, but that's all. Being here with her mother for the last years of her life would be so good. She wouldn't worry about her as much.

"That's why being a rancher is great. Especially now that I know more about what I'm doing, and I'm not so young and proud that I'm afraid to ask for help. I'm grateful for the life I've been given."

"Me too, Adrian," she said. "Me too."

They saw a jeep headed in their direction.

"Oh no, security is making its rounds. They're going to think we're crazy for sitting out here on a cold night, watching the moon and the stars."

She smiled. "I like being a little crazy."

"Yeah, me too," he said. "Come on, we better go before your mother gets worried about you."

"Adrian, I've had a really nice day. Thanks for inviting me," she said.

As his arms unfurled from around her, he glanced down, and for a moment, she thought he was going to kiss her, but then the sound of the jeep interrupted them.

"Me too, Madison. Me too," he said before he released her and hurried over to the man in the jeep.

CHAPTER 10

Tonight was the night of the engagement. They were attending one of the smaller parties at the country club and it was by invitation only.

Yesterday had left Adrian confused. The day had been the most fun he'd had in a long time, and just being with Madison was entertaining. The woman was self-reliant, happy, and confident. And when she'd kissed him in front of the other women, he'd almost lost it right there.

That kiss left him reeling with the need to pick her up and carry her home and not let her out of his bed. But that wasn't possible. That would mean another marriage and he wasn't certain he was capable of getting married again.

Last night, he'd come home to having doubts about what they were doing. Maybe he should not be pretend dating anyone. What if Madison was starting to have feelings for him? But more than anything, what if he was developing feelings for Madison?

Neither one of them could fall for the other, but he felt out of control. And that was a feeling he never wanted to experience.

Fixing the tie on his tuxedo, he glanced in the mirror and checked his pocket for the ring. He'd wanted her to wear the biggest ring he could find. Why he wanted it to be a great ring, he didn't know, but even pretending, Madison deserved the best.

Tonight had to be perfect and yet he didn't understand the pressure he was putting on himself.

This was a fake engagement. Nothing more.

Before he headed downstairs, he checked the shine on his cowboy boots and they shone with brilliance.

As he approached the kitchen, he heard Madison and her mother.

"Mom, that's perfect," Madison said.

"I don't like this," her mother replied. "I'm worried about you."

There was silence for a moment. "Nothing to worry about, Momma. I'm fine. You know how I feel about marriage."

"Which is ridiculous, but that is a discussion for another day. This just feels like a dangerous game the two of you are playing. Someone is going to get hurt," her mother said.

There was no sound, and he cleared his throat to let the ladies know he was in the kitchen.

"Are you ready?" he asked.

"Yes," she replied. "I've got to go, Momma. You worry too much."

"Have a good time," she said. "Be careful. Watch out for drunk drivers."

Madison stepped out from behind the center island and

his knees grew weak. The gown she wore was stunning. It shimmered with a gold essence that made her sapphire-gray eyes glow. Her hair and makeup were spotless. He would be the envy of every man there tonight.

"Wow," he muttered. If he ever married, she would be the type of woman he would want, but he wasn't going to say "I do". And while he'd been feeling a little wishy-washy on the subject, it sounded like Madison was certain of her feelings. Good, that went for both of them.

"A special dress for a special occasion," she said smiling.

"A special dress that will have me keeping the men away from you. I think our positions have reversed."

A grin spread across her face.

"Are you ready?"

"Yes," she said, picking up an evening shawl and purse that matched the dress.

They walked out the door and he helped her into the truck. The dress had a slit on the side, and the sight of her long, slender legs, had him swallowing down the passion that rocked through him.

When he climbed in, she reached over and picked a piece of lint off his black tux. "You look mighty handsome yourself. No wonder the women in town are chasing after you. There might be a stampede of women coming after you at the ball tonight."

He grinned at her.

"Not with you by my side," he said.

"Nope," she said confidently. "Next week is the last ball of the season," she said. "We have two more big dates and then we'll have to decide how our breakup happens and why. The season will be over and you can go back to being the most wanted bachelor in town."

He was dreading that. No, he wouldn't be in town much except to pick up supplies from the hardware store, but the thought of women pursuing him again was not fun. Already he knew that Norma Jean would try to offer to console him.

What if this didn't have to end?

The thought popped into his head, and he knew he was playing on a dangerous playground. Neither wanted marriage, but what if he could arrange a deal with her to always be his fake fiancée and be seen together in public occasionally? Would she consider the deal?

She could be like his permanent non-relationship party date. They could both help each other out.

"Tell me the plan for tonight," she said.

He didn't want to tell her. He wanted this to be spontaneous and fun.

"When the mood feels right, I'll get down on one knee," he said, suddenly feeling frustrated and he didn't know why. They had talked about this for the last couple of weeks –how he was going to not be harassed by women.

"Do we have to break up?" he blurted.

In the darkness, he could see a frown cross her face. "We only agreed to do this during the rodeo ball season."

With a sigh, he pulled into the parking lot of the country club. "I know. It's just been so convenient and I like not having women pursuing me."

She was silent. "You know I would step in and go with you whenever you need a date."

But that wasn't what he wanted, but he just thought the same thing a second ago. Right now, he didn't know what he wanted. Confusion swirled through him, and after he turned off the truck, he turned to her.

"I've enjoyed our dates. Being with you has been easy. Not having women chasing me has been wonderful. I know we only agreed to do this during the rodeo party season, but it's been nice."

She bit her lip. "It has been nice. I've had fun with you. Right now, I need to focus on moving here and getting my law practice set up."

"You could always live out at the ranch with your mother," he said.

Shaking her head, she reached out and touched his arm and desire filled him. "Thank you, but no. Everyone would believe we're living together and I want to make it on my own."

With a sigh, he opened the door of the truck and climbed out. She was right, and he hated that. What was it he wanted with Madison? No, he didn't want marriage, but he didn't want to let her go either.

He helped her out of the truck. "Let the fun begin," he said sarcastically as he took her by the hand and led her into the club.

When they walked into the ballroom, music was playing and people were dancing. They wound their way through tables until they found where they were to sit.

He grumbled when seeing they were seated at the same table as his ex-wife and her new husband. With a sigh, he pulled out Madison's chair and realized it was going to be a long night.

Leaning down, he whispered in her ear. "Are you going to be all right sitting with Laurie?"

She smiled up at him. "It's okay. What about you?"

"I hate the cheating witch, but I can be polite to her," he said. "I just want you to be comfortable."

"We'll make this work," she replied and kissed him quickly and softly on the lips.

Damn! Just that little comforting kiss set his blood on fire. It was the fact that she was concerned about him and not herself that really made him feel special.

This fake relationship was starting to feel very real and he was frightened. He loved and he hated it.

"Laurie," he said as he sat. "Chuck, how are you?"

"Doing very well," the man said.

The bastard had been sleeping with his wife in his own bed. All he'd wanted to do was deck him when he caught them, but his brother Blake had talked him down.

Even now he wanted to punch the man but would refrain. It might be an early evening.

"Do you remember Madison?" he said as he glanced at Laurie.

How had he ever thought his ex was beautiful? Compared to Madison, she was just plain.

"Hi," Laurie said, her voice strained.

"Hello," Madison said, "nice to see you again."

"You too," she said.

"Do you know Chuck?" he asked.

"No," Madison said. "I'm Madison Benton, attorney at law."

Laurie's eyes widened.

"Chuck Jones," he said.

The music stopped and the director of the rodeo stepped to

the microphone. For the next five minutes, he gave the statistics on this year's events, how many people had attended, the standings of the cowboys riding in the rodeo, and whatever else.

Beneath the table, Madison laid her hand on his leg and gave it a squeeze. He turned toward her and she smiled.

"You should be riding in the rodeo," she said. "I remember when you used to compete."

"Darling, that was a long time ago. I'm too old now," he said. "That sport is for younger men."

Laurie made a face. "He never was any good at it."

"I disagree," Madison said. "When we were in high school, he went to the state championship."

Chuck reached over and patted the back of Laurie's hand. "Now, darling, be nice. I remember Adrian being very good. Better than I ever was."

The man was trying to keep the peace while his wife was a total bitch, but Adrian was not going to let her get to him. Not when he had Madison by his side.

Their food was delivered and another couple joined them at the table which helped keep the conversation light. As soon as the dancing commenced, Adrian was going to ask the band to play a special song, and at the end, he would ask Madison to marry him.

Then after that, they were leaving. It was unfortunate that Laurie and Chuck had been seated at their table. But he was determined the two were not going to ruin this evening.

As the waitstaff were picking up the dishes, he spoke to the band leader. "I want to propose to my girlfriend. Do you know *Marry Me* by Bruno Mars?"

The man grinned. "We'll play it next."

"Thank you, and at the end of the song, I'll make an announcement," he said grinning.

Why did this feel so real? So perfect even though it was all fiction?

When he returned to the table, Madison was laughing with the woman sitting next to her. Laurie and Chuck were in a heated discussion.

The music began to play and he gazed at Madison. "Dance with me?"

"Of course," she said and he helped her from her chair.

When they reached the floor, he took her into his arms. It felt so good to hold her close. To feel her body moving in time with his. Damn, but this was getting so close to feeling real and he liked the way they were together. He liked holding her and wanted her in his bed.

Just the thought made him tense but it was time for them to once again put on a show. As the music came to an end, he pulled away from her.

"And now for something really special," the band leader said.

Dropping to one knee, Adrian took her hand in his. She lifted her other hand to her face and smiled.

"Madison, you make me feel like a whole man again. You've healed my hurts and given me joy. I never thought I would say these words ever again. Will you do me the honor of being my wife?"

She laughed and then she pulled him to his feet and laid her lips over his and kissed him deeply. When they came apart, she grinned at him. "Yes, Adrian, I would love to be your wife."

They hadn't mentioned words of love and yet he felt like they hovered in the air around them.

He took the ring out of the box and slipped it on her finger. The crowd broke into applause and he took her into his arms again.

The band began to play *All of Me* by John Legend and he pulled her closer.

She grinned at him and then leaned against him. "That was a beautiful proposal, Adrian."

"Thank you," he said. "I practiced."

A giggle came from her.

A couple danced by them. "Congratulations, you two."

When the song ended, they walked back to the table where Laurie glared at them.

"Congratulations," Chuck said.

"Yes, congratulations," she spit out. "Watch out for the prenup. He really screwed me over."

Adrian gave her a smile. He'd been more than generous with her, but she'd wanted half and he refused. That's why he'd had her sign a prenup. That money was his before he married her and it also belonged to Kissing Oaks Ranch.

"No worries," Madison said with a smile. "Remember, I'm an attorney. I don't want or need his money."

Laurie's eyes widened. "Oh my God, look at that ring. You never spent that kind of money on my ring."

He shrugged. "Only the best for Madison."

Laurie's face turned a bright red, and for a moment, Madison feared his ex-wife was going to lose it right there in the ballroom.

Madison gazed at him. "Darling, I'm ready for you to take me home and take me to bed."

A groan escaped from him. The woman was killing him. Killing him! That was exactly what he wanted to do, but their agreement did not include exploring each other's bodies.

And he longed to do nothing but peel that dress from her body and taste every inch of her.

"Let's go," he said eager to get out of there.

Rising from her chair, he wrapped the shawl around her, and she picked up her purse.

"Goodnight, everyone," she said, smiling as she laid her hand on his arm. "Take me home."

"Your wish is my command," he said, knowing that would irritate Laurie even more.

They walked away, but when they reached the door, Norma Jean was waiting for them.

"You're engaged," she said, her face red, her eyes shooting daggers at Madison.

"Yes," Madison said, holding up her ring to show her the rock. "He did so well choosing the ring."

Shaking her head, the woman stared at the two of them. "You said you were never going to marry again."

And he wasn't, but this woman didn't need to know this.

"Sometimes love has a way of winning a person over," Madison said. "And he's ridden right into my heart."

Adrian grinned at her. The woman must be an excellent attorney because she was a fine actress.

"Come on, darling, let's go home," he said.

"Yes," she replied, gazing up at him. "Goodnight, Norma Jean."

When they got into the truck, they turned and gazed at each other and burst out laughing.

"That was fun," she said. "Who knew your ex-wife would be here."

"Yes," he said laughing. But why was a small part of him already hurting knowing this would end soon?

This woman was getting to him. He liked the sound of her laughter, he loved her smile, and the touch of her hand on his was enough to send passion pouring through him. There was so much about them that he liked.

Why did this have to end?

CHAPTER 11

madison had worked all day on setting up her office. Right now, she had no receptionist, and until she had more clients, she'd not be hiring any help. The store had delivered the desk she'd chosen, and her matching file cabinets were set up. The phone company had been here and installed her landlines.

On Sunday, she started moving into the new apartment down the street from her new place of employment. She would be able to walk to work. No more driving in heavy traffic or paying every month to park downtown.

She'd filed the necessary paperwork to get her business off the ground and running and soon she would be a real bona fide lawyer's office.

The only problem was that she would now see more of Adrian than ever before and that was turning out to be a problem.

The handsome man was kind and sweet and his proposal the other night had been wonderful. Better than Randall's proposal by a long shot. And it had made her stop to think about how much she was enjoying being with him. How much she laughed when she was in his company. How comfortable they were together.

This felt way too real and that did worry her.

As her client, she shouldn't be dating him, and they would officially end their relationship after this weekend's ball, but still, this ending was going to be harder than she anticipated.

The phone rang and she jumped.

"Benton Law Firm, Madison Benton," she said smiling. It was the first time she'd received a call in her new business.

"Madison?"

The voice sounded familiar and a trickle of anger shimmered through her. Why was he calling?

"Yes," she said, knowing this was not a phone call she wanted to take.

"It's your father. I heard about your engagement to Adrian Landry. Congratulations," he said.

It was the first time he'd called since she was in school. At least a decade had passed. Why would he call her now?

"Thank you," she said suspiciously.

"It's been a long time, baby," he replied.

That's what he'd called her when she was a little girl. The memory of him saying those words and the warmth they brought her filled her with fury.

"Yes," she said. "Ten years."

"That long? It seems like only yesterday," he replied. "The next time I'm close to Oakdale, I'll stop in and see you and your own law firm. You've grown up and are doing so well for yourself."

With no help from him. Her mother had helped her as much as she could, but her father had contributed nothing to get her through college or law school. She'd worked part-time and she had student loan debts that she was slowly paying down.

"Your sisters are all in college," he said.

They weren't her sisters. They shared some DNA that he'd sown while married to her mother. She didn't want anything to do with them after the way they treated her as a child, with their mother's approval, no less.

"Denise, your second mother, is doing quite well," he said, like saying their names would interest her in them.

"How's your mother doing?"

"She's fine," she said not willing to share with him that her mother had suffered a stroke and miraculously recovered without any lasting effects. If he was phishing, he'd get nothing from her.

"So when is the wedding?" he asked.

"We haven't set a date," she replied. And no, he would never walk her down the aisle.

A sigh escaped him. "I was hoping you could help me out. Putting three girls through college is putting a strain on us and I was hoping you could lend me twenty thousand dollars since you're marrying a billionaire."

Curses filled her brain. Her body went cold before fire rushed through her and she gasped unnerved by the gall of the man.

"Excuse me" escaped from her mouth before she had time to recover. "How much did you help me when I was going to college? Who is paying for my student loans? When was the last time you paid child support?"

About three years after the divorce, he just stopped supporting his child. When her mother asked about it, he told her he'd be sending her a check next week. Only next week never came. Every time she asked, it was always *the check is in the mail.*

"Now, honey," he said. "You're marrying a very wealthy man. You could share a little of that wealth with your father."

Everything she'd learned about controlling her emotions in the courtroom disappeared. Only this man could make her training vanish.

"Like hell! It's not my money, it's Adrian's. You have a lot of nerve to call me after ten years and expect me to send you money. You may be my father by blood, but you've never been a father to me since I was a little girl and you decided your second family was more important than Mother and me."

There were other things she wanted to say to him, but she couldn't think of them as rage flowed through her brain cells igniting them. It was a wonder her hair wasn't on fire.

"Madison, I knew you were well taken care of by your mother. My family needed me," he said. "All I need is twenty thousand."

Did he not get the message?

"Yes, your other daughters needed you," she said, her voice trembling. "Tell that to the nine-year-old who stood waiting for you to pick her up after school to spend the weekend with you. You left me at school. Did you ever think that maybe I needed a father as much as they did? And then you have the nerve to call me and want me to give you my fiancé's money. People in hell will receive ice water faster than you'd get a dime from me or Adrian."

With that, she hung up the phone.

Laying her head on the desk, the tears flowed. The first time he'd called her in a decade and all he wanted was money.

Money that wasn't hers and she had no right to offer. A sob escaped her as she cried for the little girl who had lost her father. She cried for all the hard work she'd done to put herself through school with only her mother's help. She cried at the graduations he'd missed. Her high school graduation, college, and even her law school graduation. He never attended one.

And yet when he learned that she was engaged to a billion-aire rancher, he wanted twenty thousand dollars.

The front door opened and she quickly swiped the tears from her eyes. Someone had walked into her law office already.

Walking out of her office, she saw Adrian with a huge bouquet of flowers in his arms.

"Congratulations," he said, his face going from happy to one of concern. "What's wrong? Why are you crying," he asked, putting the flowers down and rushing to her.

He took her into his arms and she held on to him.

Did she dare tell him what her father had just done? Wasn't this exactly like the women who were after him for his money? And now her own family member was doing the same thing.

"Nothing," she said, the tears filling her eyes again.

Guiding her to a couch she had put in the lobby, he sat her down and took both of her hands in his.

"You're crying. Something's wrong. Tell me what upset you," he said, wiping a tear from her cheek.

With a sigh, she told him about the call with her father. When she finished, she started crying again. "I'm sorry."

"Why? It's not your fault," he said. "This is what happens when someone has a lot of money. Suddenly people come crawling out of the wood shavings looking for a handout. Twenty thousand is actually a pretty low request. Normally, they want a hundred thousand dollars."

Shaking her head, she sighed. "It's just I hadn't heard from him in so long and he calls to ask me for money. He did say *congratulations*."

"Maybe us getting fake engaged wasn't such a great idea," he said. "Now you're going to experience what I deal with on a daily basis. I didn't even think about that."

If that was a taste of what he had to deal with, then no, she didn't want a billion dollars. She didn't want people calling her and begging for money. Her father was an easy person to turn down, but what if someone had a dire need for cash? What would she do then?

The phone rang and she was afraid to answer. What if it was him again?

Slowly, she reached for the phone sitting on the receptionist's desk.

"Benton Law Firm, Madison Benton," she said.

"How dare you hang up on your father like that," her stepmother Denise said. "We need that cash."

Taking a deep breath, what she'd learned in school took over. This one was easier to deal with since she'd never liked the woman.

"Hello, Denise, how are you? I hear your daughters are all in college," she said.

"We need that money to keep them in school," she said. "You've got plenty now that you're marrying a rich man."

These two people deserved one another. And yet, she had her father's DNA. But she would never be like him. She would never be anything like these two welches.

"Oh, you've heard about my engagement," she said, calmly thinking the woman hadn't even said congratulations, just she wanted money.

"You know, I have so many school loans to pay off because I didn't receive any help getting through college or law school. Mother and I have made it on our own for many years without my father's child support. And yet the first time you hear I'm marrying a wealthy man, you two call and want money."

"Uh, the years just got away from us," she said. "We've been busy raising our daughters."

"Of course, I completely understand. But I will tell you like I told dear old Dad, it's Adrian's money, not mine. I'll tell you like Dad always told Mom, the check is in the mail. It was great talking to you. Have a wonderful life."

Click. She hung up the phone. When she turned to Adrian, he busted out laughing.

"Damn, one day I'm going to come see you in court. I bet you can tear up a witness with your subtle questioning."

With a sigh, she pushed back her blonde hair. "I'm sorry. I never thought they would call to ask for money. That takes a lot of gall. My father is the reason I never want to marry or have children. I come from his blood and what if I become like him?"

Adrian shook his head. "No, you're nothing like your father. And you never will be."

"Did you know that he created a second family while he was married to my mother? Then after they divorced, he would pick me up and take me to spend the weekend with them. Where Denise would mistreat me when he wasn't look-ing. Though the girls were only a year or two younger than me, they enjoyed being mean to me. One time, I stood outside school waiting for him to pick me up and he never showed. No call. Nothing. After that, I never went to his other home again."

Adrian pulled her into his arms and she cried against his shoulder. "I'm sorry."

"Shhh, you have no reason for being sorry. He was a terrible father," he said. "I can't imagine being left at school. What kind of father does that?"

"A lousy one," she said. "Because of him, I'm afraid of marriage. What if the man I marry left me and created a second family? What if he never saw our children or paid their child support? I can't take a chance on getting married."

Leaning down, he kissed the top of her head and she clung to him, enjoying the feel of his chest against hers.

"Come on, I'm taking you to dinner tonight," he said. "We're going to celebrate you opening your law firm. We'll laugh and have fun and forget about the call from my future degenerate father-in-law. You did tell them they would not be invited to the wedding?"

She leaned back in his arms and saw he was teasing. Laughter filled her chest. He made her feel better.

"No, I forgot, but they wouldn't be," she said. "Thank you for bringing me flowers. That means a lot to me."

"You're welcome. Now come on, we need to add some water to them and then we'll go," he said. "Let's celebrate."

CHAPTER 12

It was their last date. Their last ball, and after tonight, they would figure out a way to break their engagement. And yet the last two months had been the most fun he'd had in years.

Being with Madison felt right and he fought his need for her. He didn't want to need any woman, and this one was the hardest of anyone he'd ever dated. She fit him just right and that scared him.

As of this week, Madison had her law practice up and running, she'd moved into her new apartment, and even had her first client besides him. Everything was falling into place for her and he was glad. He'd even helped her move her furniture into her new place and liked the fact she could walk back and forth to her office.

And the way she'd handled her father and stepmother had impressed him. Sure, having her father call asking for money after not seeing her for ten years had hurt her, but her stepmother had just angered her. Not to mention he wanted to call on them and tell the bastard to never call her again, but that wasn't his right.

Yet, the urge to protect Madison overwhelmed him.

He felt guilty because he had never thought about people calling her and asking her for his money. And yet she had his back. She'd turned them down so fast, the telephone line was still probably crackling from her hitting the disconnect button.

The wind outside howled and he wondered if they should go tonight. They were predicting sleet later and they would need to keep an eye on the weather to make certain they got home before the ice storm arrived.

Of course, Texas weathermen had predicted the worst before, and they hadn't even received a drop. But you didn't want to have to slip and slide home either.

Tonight's shindig was in Fort Worth which was an hour away. He'd thought about hiring a limo driver but decided it would be better if he took his truck. That way, they could leave whenever they were ready. Plus, he had four-wheel drive if the weather did get dicey.

Waiting for her in the living room, he stood with his heavy coat and gloves. It was already colder than a witch in Montana and they were used to the cold weather.

His brothers told him they had moved the cattle to the closest pasture and had put out plenty of hay and water with more available first thing in the morning.

The pipes outside of the house were covered. They were as prepared as they could be if they did receive this ice storm. But most of the time, the jet stream flowed farther to the east and not so much south.

She walked into the room and his eyes widened at the

sight of her in a blue gown that made her light blue-gray eyes sparkle. The gown fit her curves and hers were all in the right place.

Damn, the woman was gorgeous and he wondered why he'd never considered dating her before now.

"If you get any prettier, I'm going to have to hire you bodyguards," he said.

She smiled. "You are such a flatterer. Keep saying such nice things, but it's not going to get you anywhere."

That was the problem; he wanted more. A lot more, but there was this no-marriage thing standing between them. And he was as much to blame as she was.

After hearing about her father and listening to the conversation with her stepmom, he understood her feelings about matrimony. Yet what they had felt real. It was comfortable in some ways with a dash of fire sparking between them.

"Are you ready?"

"You both be careful," her mother said. "The weather is supposed to turn nasty."

"We'll be back early if it starts sleeting," he said. Not really wanting this night to be short because this was the end.

As much as he hated it, he didn't think she would take a chance on them dating for real.

Tonight, she was taking her big coat and he helped her slip into the long fur-lined jacket. It would be warmer than the shawl she normally wore.

"Goodnight," her mother called and Madison took his hand in hers.

They walked out to the truck without saying a word and he helped her up.

"I thought about hiring a limo tonight, but decided we'd

have better luck in the truck, especially if we decided to leave early."

Turning to her, he pulled the gift he'd bought her on a whim out of his pocket.

"I got you this," he said, handing her the small, wrapped box.

Her eyes widened. "Why?"

"Because I wanted to," he said, wanting something for her to remember him by.

She peeled the paper away and opened the box that contained a tennis bracelet encircled in diamonds. Yes, he'd spent some money on it, but she was worth every penny.

"No, Adrian. I can't accept this."

"I bought it because I wanted you to have it. It's something to remember our time together by."

"It's too much," she said. "And I'll never forget our time together. It's been way more than I ever expected."

"Me too," he said. "Please, I want you to have it."

Reaching up she pulled his face to hers and gave him a brief kiss on the lips. Oh, how he wanted so much more than that simple touch. And he wanted those kisses not to be fake but real. Real with meaning and feelings behind them.

"Thank you," she said, "but you've already given me so much. My law practice is going because of you and the new client I received this week."

"Good," he said. "I'm glad you're here."

He started the engine and they were on their way. It took them less than an hour to reach Fort Worth with little traffic. When a winter storm was predicted, most people stayed home.

He pulled up in front of the hotel where the event was

taking place and valet parked. Handing a young man the keys, he got out of the truck.

Then he walked around and helped Madison alight from the truck. She left her coat in the vehicle and he noted she was cold as they hurried inside the hotel.

"This place is beautiful," she said.

Tonight, they would hand out the trophies and cash prizes to all the cowboys who had won the different divisions of the rodeo.

Leading her into the ballroom, they were shown to their table. Thank goodness tonight they were not placed next to his cheating ex and her husband.

For over an hour, they sat and listened to awards being handed out while they ate the delicious dinner. Finally, the music began to play and he led her onto the floor to dance.

He wanted to hold her for as long as possible and share as many dances as he could with her. This was the last ball of the season and he had no need for her to protect him from the overzealous women any longer.

And yet he didn't want it to end.

"What if we continued to see each other," he said as they glided across the floor. She felt so good in his arms but the moment he said those words, she tensed.

"I don't think that's a good idea," she said.

"Why not?" he asked.

She bit her lip. "Because sooner or later, one of us will develop feelings for the other and then we'll both end up hurt. Because you haven't changed your mind on marriage and neither have I. In fact, hearing from my father this week confirmed what I knew. Marriage is not good for me."

While he knew what she was saying was true, that didn't mean he didn't want to see her any longer.

"We're having fun. Why can't we continue to keep things light and casual?" he said.

"For the reasons I just outlined," she replied.

Suddenly they heard tapping on the glass panes on the ceiling of the ballroom.

It was sleeting. Damn, for once, the weathermen were right.

"We need to leave," he said.

She grabbed her purse off the table and they hurried to the valet stand.

Other people were doing the same, and there was a line of people waiting to get their cars. The poor guys were doing their best to get people their vehicles, but it was a madhouse.

Standing inside the hotel, Adrian watched as Norma Jean approached.

"Seasons over," she said, glancing between the two of them. "When's the wedding?"

Adrian didn't want to talk to this woman or any other woman right now. He wanted Madison.

"We're just enjoying being together," Madison told her. "We're going to wait awhile."

The woman smiled. "Or you're going to break up and I'll have my chance at him again."

Adrian felt Madison tense beside him. "Oh, Norma Jean, I feel truly sorry for you. Adrian is mine and will be until the end of time."

The words sank into him, and he realized he wanted to be hers until the end of time. In the two months they'd dated, he'd fallen in love with this saucy woman and he'd even agree to marry her if that would keep her by his side.

"Darlin', they just pulled the truck up. Be safe gettin' home, Norma Jean," he said as he helped Madison out the door.

When they were both safely buckled in, he began the treacherous drive. The sleet was really coming down.

He felt the back tires of the truck slide and eased off the gas.

"Whoa," Madison said.

The sound of ice pellets was loud as they drove through downtown Fort Worth.

"Hopefully, this will stop when we reach the south side of town."

They were both quiet as he concentrated on driving.

They hit the interstate and traffic came to a dead stop.

"We might have been better to spend the night at the hotel," Madison said.

"Maybe."

After an hour of being in the truck, the traffic began to slowly move. It was past midnight and the sleet had not let up. The ground was turning white. They were going so slow, it would be morning before they arrived at the Kissing Oaks Ranch.

He hit the brakes to stop and the truck slid sideways. He managed to stop before he hit the vehicle in front of him, but he quickly reached a decision.

"Find us a hotel. We're not going to make it home tonight," he said. "We're getting off the highway and out of the weather."

She sighed and grabbed her phone. "There's a hotel at the next exit."

It took them another twenty minutes to reach the exit and he had never been so glad to get off that interstate.

They pulled up in front under the cover and he hurried her inside.

It wasn't a bad-looking place, but he saw from the number of cars in the front that they were busy. Everyone on the highway was doing the same as them. Seeking shelter from the storm.

"Do you have two rooms," he asked.

The clerk behind the desk shook his head. "I only have one, but it says there are two queen beds."

"We'll take it," he said, not looking at her.

She didn't argue with him and he knew she had been just as nervous as he was while sitting on that interstate.

"Good thing you got off the highway," the clerk told him as Adrian paid for the room. "The interstate is closed about a mile down the road. We've been talking to our sister hotel down the way and they have sold out of all their rooms."

He'd made the right decision.

"Thank you," he said, turning to Madison. "Why don't you go on up to the room and I'll park the truck."

"All right," she said and he could see she was nervous.

Quickly, he secured the truck in one of the last spots available.

Before he went upstairs, he searched around the hotel for food or drinks. All he found were some candy bars, popcorn, and soda.

Not exactly what he wanted. He would've loved to have a beer or a cocktail, anything to prepare him for sharing a room with Madison for the night.

With his hands loaded down with junk food to keep his

mind off her sleeping in the room with him, he stepped into the elevator.

At the room's door, he quietly knocked.

When she opened up, she stared at him with surprise. "Are you hungry?"

It was all he could do to keep from saying, *only for you*. But he smiled and stepped into the room.

There was only one bed.

"I thought it was two beds," he said.

"Me too," she replied, gazing at him, her sapphire eyes large.

"I'll sleep on the floor," he replied, setting the snacks on a small table in the room.

"No, you will not," she said. "Look at the floor. It's not nasty, but it's not clean either. We'll find a way to make this work."

"Did you call your mother?"

"Yes," she said. "She told me it's coming down hard there and we were smart to stay in town."

That was a two-edged sword. It was smart to get off the road, but to spend the night together in a hotel room when all he could think about was getting her to change her mind about the two of them wasn't the brightest idea he'd ever had.

He'd fallen in love with this woman and they were in a very precarious situation.

"They had a little stand downstairs with extra toothbrushes and toothpaste," he said. "I bought us each one."

Handing her a toothbrush, she sighed. "This is weird."

"Yes," he said.

"It's our last date, and here we are in a hotel room, spending the night."

They had no nightclothes, and he was not about to sleep in his tuxedo, and she could not sleep in her evening gown.

What would she wear?

"You can sleep in my shirt," he said.

"Thanks."

They were both nervous and felt awkward. It had never felt like this between them before.

"I'll use the bathroom first and then you can change into my shirt," he said, walking into the small bath.

Quickly, he brushed his teeth and removed the tux coat and his shirt. He was going to leave his pants on until they went to bed and then once the lights were out, he'd remove them.

When he walked out of the bathroom, he handed her the shirt.

"Here you go," he said.

A few minutes later he heard her brushing her teeth and then he heard her struggling.

She opened the door and stared at him. "I can't get the zipper down on this dress. Can you help me?"

Oh God, did she know what she was asking him to do and yet he couldn't refuse her.

"Yes," he said in a quiet whisper.

Turning her back to him, she lifted her hair off her neck and he gazed at her bare back. The dress was strapless and her hair had hidden that gorgeous expanse of her neck and back.

Easing the zipper down, he couldn't stop himself when he leaned down and his lips kissed her neck and then found their way down her back.

She sighed and a shiver ran through her.

"Adrian," she gasped.

Whirling her around, the dress dropped to the floor and she stood before him in a thong and strapless bra. All that expanse of pure silky skin was before him.

She was beautiful. So damn gorgeous and he couldn't resist her any longer.

He layered his mouth over hers and kissed her like he'd wanted to for weeks. His mouth conveyed what his body yearned for, and he couldn't resist pulling her against him wanting her to feel what she did to him.

This was not fake. This was the real deal.

But if she didn't want this, he would never force himself on her.

Leaning back, he gazed into her eyes. "Madison," he said with all the longing consuming him.

"Are you sure about this?"

"Shut up and fuck me," she said. "I need you, Adrian."

as she crazy?

When she walked into the room, the sight of that big empty bed sent images of the two of them naked beneath the sheets and exploring each other's body surging through her brain.

And then Adrian walked in the door and her heart skipped a beat. At the thought of sleeping beside him, she knew she was in trouble. Especially after he made the suggestion that they continue dating.

She couldn't. But her heart was already involved, and after tonight, the tentacles of love would be wrapped around her, demanding that she do everything in her power to stay with him no matter what her head told her.

Blood roared in Madison's ears as she leaned into Adrian's kiss, unable to resist the pull of his attraction any longer. The realization that she cared for this man left her feeling reckless. Coupled with the ball tonight, the gift he'd given her, and the engagement ring she wore, she was defenseless against her unbearable need to be in his arms. And she could no longer fight the feelings she had for this man.

Somewhere along their journey, she'd fallen in love with this sweet, kind cowboy.

Consequences be damned, she was hungry for the feel of his body entwined around hers, delirious with wanting him, desperate to be possessed by Adrian.

While his mouth plundered hers, she returned his feverous kisses with fierceness that surprised her.

This wasn't their first passionate kiss, but it was the one that mattered. This kiss was not fake or for show. This kiss expressed the emotions she had for him. Placing her hands on his face, she molded his lips to hers, opening to receive him. Sweet, sinful sensations erupted in a delicious soft moan that escaped from the back of her throat.

They would have no tomorrows, but they had tonight.

His hands gripped her shoulders as though he would never let her go, his lips commanded her surrender as he guided her back until her legs bumped into the bed. That big, empty bed they would soon occupy. He leaned into his kiss, pressing his arousal through her thong into the V of her legs. From the feel of his muscular thighs to the strength of his sinewy chest, she felt all of him. Every delicious, rock-hard inch.

While she was almost naked, he still had way too many clothes on.

Since the very beginning of their dates, she had fought the way their bodies seemed to be drawn to each other. All it took was an ice storm, and in a weak moment, he managed to overcome her defenses.

She slid her hands over his shoulders, down his muscled

back, past his waist, until she gripped his buttocks, melding them even more firmly together.

Oh, how she wanted this. How she'd dreamed of being in his arms. Her mind was screaming warnings while her body demanded he take her. Tonight, she was shutting off the rational part of her brain and experiencing what she'd secretly longed for.

She was past the point of control. Nothing could stop her from being with this man, not even the risk of losing her heart to him. Not even the chance of him walking away and leaving her behind.

Tomorrow would be soon enough to deal with the consequences.

She was tired of fighting these sensations. She wanted Adrian.

He moaned, his tongue tracing the ridges of her lips, his kiss turning savage as she held him tightly against her, intoxicating her with desire. Nothing mattered at this moment except this man, this kiss, and the feel of his body taut with need for her, only her.

Adrian made her feel alive. He made her feel things she tried to resist. He made her feel like a woman. No other man had ever made her feel the way he did.

His lips moved to her throat.

"Madison," he moaned, his voice husky.

Her hands skimmed his naked chest. "You have way too many clothes on," she said.

She wanted to touch him, make him as giddy with passion as she felt. Tonight, she needed Adrian. She was tired of being his make-believe fiancée.

Letting her fingertips guide her, she traced the hardened

muscles of his chest, touching every solid ridge. For two months, she'd felt the strength of his broad shoulders, but never been able to experience the feel of his flesh.

Why couldn't she put him out of her mind instead of craving his touch? Why couldn't she walk away from the cowboy and just let their time together end without tonight?

Because no matter what, he made her feel complete in ways she'd never experienced. With just one smoldering glance, her senses quivered in anticipation.

Neither of them had planned on taking their game this far, but somewhere along the road, it became real. At least for her.

"Madison," he moaned, his lips covering hers once more. As their kiss deepened, his fingers deftly unhooked the strapless bra she'd worn beneath her dress. The cool night air brushed her skin, and she felt a moment of panic. What was she doing?

This wasn't supposed to happen.

And then his lips touched the sensuous part of her neck, causing her to shiver. His lips trailed the material down her chest, nipping her in the curvature of her shoulder. A shudder passed through her as his lips seared a path down to her breasts.

She leaned her head back, giving him full access to her body. She was crazy with want for him, and at this moment, nothing else mattered. Her breathing was fast and shallow as she reached for the snap on his tuxedo pants.

"Wait, Madison," he whispered as he sank down on the bed and tugged his boots off, kicking them across the room. Then he reached for his pants and quickly undid them while she stepped out of her thong. Rising, he stood naked, all male before her. His manhood protruded before him, smooth, long, and hard. With a decisive pang, her heart filled with passion and she realized it was too late.

He grabbed her shoulders and pushed her back onto the bed, following her down. With a seductive cry, she reached out and touched his face, her hand caressing his cheek and pulling him toward her. "I want you."

Her lips expressed what her heart knew and her voice could not say as she covered his mouth with hers and became lost in the sensation of his lips.

There were no future promises, but there was the pleasure of now.

"Thank God, you do," he whispered, nipping the curvature of her neck.

His lips trailed down to her breasts, and his mouth closed over her nipple, laving the bud until she gripped his head, her breathing harsh.

His one hand skimmed her body, sending quivers through her, while his other delved into the center of her femininity. She jerked at the unexpected jolt of pleasure that rippled through her. She wanted him desperately, yet she was afraid.

"I'm going to tease you until you beg me to stop," he gasped, breathing hard to fill his lungs.

Madison moaned, the sound loud and voracious in the darkened room. She arched against his hand, gripping the sheets against the raging need his fingers were building with his caresses.

"Please," she said while his fingers teased and tormented her. Never had a man with just the touch given her such pleasure. Never had she experienced this ache that let her know she needed him.

"Adrian!" she cried as she tensed, trying to hold on to the

sweeping pleasure that descended on her as she disintegrated beneath his hands.

For a moment, she lay there, her breathing hard and quick, her eyes closed while she slowly collected herself. Then the feel of Adrian thoroughly aroused and lying beside her caught her attention.

She opened her eyes and gazed at him, knowing this night would forever change them. His eyes were dark, hungry, filled with passion for her and so beautiful, she had to resist the urge to kiss each one.

She didn't want to love him and didn't want to experience these emotions. But there was no denying he made her feel wonderful. He made her laugh, and he made her feel special, but most of all, he made her feel so loved. And there was no denying she had fallen for him.

Her hand slid past his waist, teasing him, getting just close enough to brush her fingers across the tip of his manhood. She gazed at him and watched as anticipation rippled across his face.

"My big, strong cowboy," she said softly, goading him. Wanting him inside her.

Finally, she wrapped her hand around his rock-hard shaft. She gently slid her palm over the tip and then wrapped her fingers around him. She stroked the hot, smooth length, gripping until he grabbed her hand.

Rolling himself on top of her, he caught and held both of her hands high above her head.

She writhed beneath him, teasing him with her body when her hands could not do the job.

Slowly he slid his body over her breasts, her thighs, still holding her hands captive in his own.

"Enough, Madison," he whispered, his husky voice sending tremors down her spine. "It's past time for me to feel you wrapped around me. It's past time for me to fuck you."

His knees nudged open her thighs, his hands released her wrists and gripped her waist as he brought her hips up to meet him and he entered her in a single thrust.

She moaned, the sound loud in the hotel room as he thrust into her welcoming body.

"Adrian," she cried unable to contain the passion their bodies were creating.

"Do you want me to stop?" he asked, staring at her, his gaze hard and unwavering.

"Not until I die," she said as she rose to meet each thrust.

He delved into her rhythmically, filling her, melding to her when she clutched him, relishing in the feel of his flesh against hers.

With each thrust, his moans filled places deep within her heart that had been empty for so very long. He opened his eyes, staring at her, filling her soul as well as her body with sweetness and contentment that had long been denied. A pleasure that even now was rushing toward her, unstoppable.

Clinging to him, Madison could feel the passion building within her. She cried out in satisfaction as her body went rigid, spasms of desire rippling through her. Cascading shivers of delight left her holding onto Adrian while he reached his own climax, shuddering, gripping her, as he found pleasure.

Madison breathed deeply the musky scent of Adrian and pressed her lips to the inside of his neck between gasps for air. She was completely spent as she lay relaxed, sated, and more confused than ever by the sensations Adrian generated.

Adrian's breathing was fast and shallow as he leaned against her. For several minutes, they lay in each other's arms, their breathing slowly returning to normal.

"Damn, Madison," he said softly.

"Hmm," she said, lying in his arms, spent, never having experienced sex like that. Never.

There in the darkness, listening as the weather took a turn for the worse, she knew she was in trouble.

"Madison, I just want you to know that I'm—"

"Stop," she said. "Let's just enjoy this time together. We're stuck in a hotel room while a storm rages outside. Let's not think about tomorrow. Only tonight."

She was in so much turmoil, she didn't want to talk about the implications of this night. Right now, she wanted to savor this moment to remember and enjoy when the heartache came. And it would come roaring for her very soon.

Rising onto his elbow, he gazed down at her. "Sometimes, you can be a real pain in the ass."

She laughed to diffuse the situation. "I'm a woman. That's my job."

"Since that was so good, I'm ready to go again," she said, staring up into his emerald eyes growing dark with passion once more.

All she wanted was to enjoy this man, because tomorrow… tomorrow, there would be pain. Lots of pain. And she wasn't ready to think about that just yet.

CHAPTER 14

The ice storm was one of the worst in history. It held the metroplex hostage for two days. And there was nothing either of them could do but stay in that hotel room.

Most of the time they were in bed, trying to keep warm by making love. The heater was not the best, and the freezing temperatures kept the room on the cold side. Plus, they didn't have any clothes but their evening wear.

On the second day, it occurred to Madison that they had not been using condoms. And in fact, they had no condoms. It was early enough in her cycle that she thought they were safe but it was still a terrifying thought.

This morning, she'd awakened early to the sound of a large diesel engine in the hotel parking lot. Jumping out of bed, she hurried to the window to see a big rig tractor-trailer pulling out. The roads were wet with an icy sheen, but the temperature had warmed overnight, and today, they would be going home day.

Today would be the day that Adrian would want to talk

and she wasn't ready. She couldn't face either of them saying that it had been fun, but it was over.

Looking at Adrian curled up in bed sleeping, fear cinched her heart. She'd fallen in love with this man, and she couldn't imagine how they could say good-bye. In fact, she didn't want to have him drop her off at her apartment and say *see you around*.

That would cheapen everything about the last two months.

He didn't want to marry and neither did she and she was not the type of woman who could sleep with a man without her feelings being involved. Glancing about, she found her evening gown and put her clothes on.

Gathering her things, she wondered how she could get out of here without Adrian knowing.

Picking up her coat and her evening purse, she quietly opened the hotel door and hurried out.

Her cell phone was almost dead. But she quickly found the number she was looking for.

"Desiree, how is the weather there?"

"It's clearing up. How are you?"

"I'm in trouble," she said tears filling her eyes. "I'm in so much trouble. I'm at a hotel in Burleson. The roads look like they've cleared. Would you mind coming to get me?"

She started to cry.

"I'm on my way," she said. "It will take me about thirty minutes to get there or longer if the roads are still icy."

"There is a restaurant down the road. I'll be waiting there," she said, thinking she could walk there to get away from Adrian.

Right now, she needed some time.

"See you soon," Desiree said.

"Thank you," she replied.

As soon as she disconnected the phone, she went to the desk clerk.

"Could I leave a written message for the man in room three twenty-three?"

"Of course," the woman said, gazing at her like she'd lost her mind.

She looked like a fancy hooker in her evening gown.

The woman handed her a pen and paper and she quickly penned Adrian a note.

I had to get away. We agreed that there would be no commitments between us and every minute I spend with you is making me doubt everything we said. Please don't try to find me. I'm headed home. Thank you for a wonderful two months. I'm sorry. Madison.

A tear slipped down her cheek. She put the note in an envelope and sealed it. Wrote Adrian's name on the front and then she handed it back to the clerk.

"Thank you," she said.

With a sigh, she put on her coat and glanced out at the sidewalks.

"Is it still icy?"

"Yes, in some spots," the woman said.

The restaurant was a block away. Taking her time, she walked as quickly as she dared in her heels. When she safely reached the restaurant, she felt relieved stepping inside the building.

The woman at the entrance gazed at her like she was a streetwalker.

"Well, good morning," the woman seating customers said. "Looks like you've had an interesting night?"

"Try three days," she said already missing Adrian and suddenly doubting her decision.

Part of her felt like she was running from something really good while the other part told her she was protecting herself. And yet, she felt like she'd left her heart in that hotel room.

"Breakfast?"

She was hungry. Two days of living on the little food the hotel had left her starving for something substantial. And yet, her heart wasn't really in the mood for a big breakfast.

"Yes," she said. "Mainly coffee."

The woman sat her at a table and then poured her a cup of coffee.

Sitting there, she watched as Adrian came out of the hotel, jumped in his truck, and tore out of the parking lot.

What had she done?

Was this the right path or should she have waited for him knowing it would be an awkward good-bye?

She ordered toast and scrambled eggs.

Just as she finished, Desiree texted her she was in the parking lot.

It was then she saw the text from her father. How he'd gotten her cell number, she didn't know, but she didn't need his nonsense right now.

We need to talk. Urgent. If you don't help me, I'll go bankrupt.

With a sigh, she texted Desiree she was coming right out. Then she paid her bill and walked out the door.

When she stepped into Desiree's SUV, her friend's brows rose.

"This is a story I need to hear," she said.

Tears welled in her eyes.

As they drove toward Oakdale, Madison filled Desiree in

on the last forty-eight hours. Of how she'd done this to help Adrian and ended up falling in love with him. And neither one of them wanted to marry.

"Oh, come on, Madison. If you love the man, why won't you take a chance on marrying him?"

She'd asked herself that question. "Because he's been married once and it didn't work out. And look at my family situation. My father had a second family while he was married to my mother. He cheated on her. My ex-fiancé cheated on me. What if Adrian cheats on me?"

"No," Desiree said. "His wife cheated on him. She was the one at fault."

"Men cheat," she said, remembering her mother crying when she'd learned of her father's second family.

Her father's blood ran through her veins. Maybe she would be the one to step out on Adrian.

After Randall cheated on her, she'd made the decision never to marry. Never to give anyone the chance to hurt her like her father had hurt her mother.

"Many of my cousins have found their mates, and I think if you're happy, you don't want to hurt the person you love. Obviously, your father wasn't happy, and he cheated on your mother. Does Adrian make you happy?"

"Yes," she said with a sigh. "Very much. But he also doesn't want to get married. Women are after his money, and he said he wasn't going to take another chance on marriage."

They rode along in silence.

"You do remember that Eugenia told you that you would marry him," Desiree said.

Eugenia? Then she remembered. The ghost.

"Look, I know you believe in her, but I'm not taking the advice of a ghost," she said. "I don't believe in them."

Desiree laughed. "You sound just like the men in my family. They don't believe in her until she finds them the love of their life. She didn't find yours, but she did tell you that you were going to marry him."

"No, I'm not marrying any man," she said. "I'm going back to Oakdale and getting busy on making my law practice successful. And no, I won't fake date any man ever again. I didn't expect it to be this hard. I didn't expect to fall in love with him."

Desiree reached over and patted her arm.

"I think I'm glad I haven't found love yet," she said with a sigh. "It's not all fun and roses like the movies make it out to be."

"No, it's not," she said, wondering how she could ever see her mother again without running into Adrian.

They pulled into town, and soon, they were in front of the small apartment she'd rented. She was home. Safe and sound and she couldn't wait to get out of this dress she'd been wearing for three days.

It was going in the trash. Too many memories were associated with the silk gown.

"Thank you for bringing me home, letting me cry on your shoulder, and listening to my sad tale of woe," she said. "I owe you a big steak dinner."

"What are friends for?" Desiree said. "Someday it could be me calling you."

"Anytime," Madison said, stepping out of the SUV.

"Be careful, it's still icy out there," Desiree said.

"You too," she replied and shut the door. She glanced up at

her apartment and wondered if she'd made a mistake quitting her job in Dallas and moving here.

Waving to Desiree, she hurried up the stairs. When she reached the top, Adrian was sitting there at the door waiting for her.

Gulping, she glanced at him. The handsome man's face was red. He was furious.

CHAPTER 15

After the best two days of his life, he'd awakened this morning to an empty bed, an empty room, and a broken heart. He'd known immediately when she wasn't in the room that she'd run.

When he reached downstairs, the desk clerk handed him her note and he'd left.

Damn her for running and not talking about what happened between them.

Damn her for making him worry about how she'd gotten home, if she was safe, or if some asshole had picked her up.

When he'd seen Desiree pulling up to the apartment building, he'd known Madison was safe, but still he wanted to speak to her.

"What are you doing here?" she asked.

"I'm making sure you got home safe and sound. And now we're going to talk," he said.

"There's nothing to talk about. Our verbal contract ended the night of the ball," she said. "It's over. We're done."

Her words infuriated him. Didn't she see what they had

was special? He'd never experienced this kind of love with Laurie. He'd never felt so close to another human being. And she wanted to destroy it all.

She put the key in her lock and opened the door. For a moment, he feared she was going to shut him outside.

"There's nothing left to say," she said.

"The hell there isn't," he said, walking in behind her.

"What are you so afraid of?" he asked her.

Turning she glared at him. "Me? I'm not the only one who doesn't want marriage."

"You're right," he said. "I'm afraid. But I thought we could try dating for real and see if this thing between us is worth pursuing."

His heart clenched. Yes, he wanted to marry her. He'd do it tomorrow if she would give him even half the chance. She'd changed him for the better. Madison was a good woman. And no, he didn't want anyone else.

"I'm not good marriage material," she said. "My father cheated on my mother. It's in my genes."

"You're not your father," he said, wondering where this had all come from.

"You don't know that," she said. "I may be just like my mother and he cheated on her. My ex-fiancé cheated on me. You could cheat on me."

He laughed. "From someone who has been cheated on, I can promise you that would never happen. It sucks. It's painful. If I'm not happy, I would seek out marital counseling before I would ever leave. But why are we talking about this? Why can't we just date for a while and see if this is what we want."

She swallowed. "No, I can't. We agreed to fake dating. That is now over and we're done."

Stepping in close to her, he lifted her chin with his finger and gazed into her eyes. "Tell me that the last two days have meant nothing to you. Tell me that you didn't enjoy yourself as much as I did. Tell me that you have no feelings for me and I'll go quietly."

She swallowed and tears formed in the corners of her eyes.

"No, it was just a fling. If we had not gotten trapped, it would never have happened."

Surprised, he stared at her and shook his head. In the last two days, he'd realized he'd fallen in love with her. He'd realized that he wanted more than just two months of being with her. He wanted it all.

And yet she was denying that she'd felt anything at all. Maybe she was unable to feel anything for anyone.

Stepping back, he knew he needed to leave. It was over.

"I'm glad you made it home safely. Thanks for the best two months of my life. You actually made me whole again. Laurie had left a pit in my heart. I hated women. I never wanted to feel anything ever again, and you showed me I could find happiness. Thank you. See you around."

With that, he walked out the door. Hurrying down the stairs, he reached his truck and climbed inside.

"Damn!" he said as he sat there, emotions raging through him. "Damn. That was not how I wanted this to end."

He backed out of the parking lot and drove home, wiping the tears that rolled down his cheeks. Why couldn't he be the one to find an everlasting love? Why?

This time, he thought he had found a forever love, only to be disappointed once again.

CHAPTER 16

The next week was hell. First, her father called her and begged for money. When she told him she was no longer engaged or seeing Adrian, he'd cursed her and called her every kind of fool.

And she had just listened to him and even agreed with him before she told him that she hoped it would be another ten years before she heard from him again.

On Sunday, her mother stopped in to see her.

"What happened between you and Adrian?" she asked.

She gave her a brief synopsis of how things ended between them.

"Madison, you're a smart woman. What makes you think you'll be like your father?"

"I don't know," she said. "I'm just not willing to take a chance on marriage and having children, and then find out one of us is cheating. The kids will have to spend every other weekend with the other parent. The new spouse will mistreat them and I'm not going to put my kids in that kind of situation."

Her mother sighed. "I had no idea that your father's new wife was so cruel. As soon as you told me, I told him you would not be returning there. That if he wanted to see you, he would need to make other arrangements. I didn't realize he would just drop off the face of the earth."

Madison started laughing. "Oh no, Mom. He's still around."

She told her about how he had been calling her and that he wanted Adrian to give him thousands of dollars. How he put his wife up to calling her and demanding the cash.

With a sigh, her mother shook her head. "I'm sorry, Madison. You were the best thing out of that marriage. And I won't lie to you and say that marriage is easy, but you are your own person. The mistakes you make in life are yours to make and no one else's. Don't shortchange your life because of what happened between me and your father. If I hadn't married, I would not have you. And you are the best thing in my life."

Tears spilled down Madison's cheeks as she stared at her mother. Was she making a mistake not taking a chance with Adrian?

"Adrian is a good man who was hurt deeply by his wife's infidelity. But between the two of you, I saw something I didn't see with him and Laurie. He cares deeply about you. And I think you enjoyed him. Is it love? I don't know. But don't be afraid of loving someone just because of me and your father."

Her mother stood and hugged her. "Whatever you decide, you know I'll support you. Now I'm going to get back to the ranch. I've been really tired today and I want to get supper cooked and then rest."

Madison nodded. "Why are you so tired?"

"Because I'm getting old," her mother said with a smile.

"Maybe it's time for you to retire. You could move into town with me and we could get a small house to rent."

Shaking her head, her mother hugged her. "No, you need to live your life. I'll be all right. I just need to rest more."

Madison watched as she walked out the door.

"Talk to you later, love you," she said.

As her mother closed the door, she thought about what her mother had said. Yes, her father had screwed up their lives, but they had each other, and if her mother hadn't married her father, then Madison would not be here.

Was she being too hard on herself? The image of Adrian swam before her and she squeezed her eyes shut.

Oh, how she missed hearing his laughter, his voice, the way he treated her. How in two months had they gone from being just acquaintances to being good friends and even lovers?

It was early afternoon and she and Desiree were going to have that steak tonight.

Rushing to get ready, she hurried out the door. After an hour, Madison stepped inside the reception building where her friend waited. The smell of lavender filled the air.

"Eugenia, not here," Desiree said. "A guest could walk in."

"Do you think I give a rat's *patatoe* about your guests?" the woman said, shimmering in the air. "I need to speak to Madison."

This was so strange. And she didn't dare tell anyone about these encounters, because if she did, they would lock her up. She'd be known as the crazy woman lawyer in Oakdale.

"Yes, Eugenia," she said not really believing she was speaking to a ghost. She looked around the room for a camera, a machine, anything that could put her image into the room.

"You're being unreasonable," Eugenia said. "You are not your father."

"Did you tell her our discussion," she said glancing at Desiree.

"No, I did not," she said. "I don't tell her much because that information can and will be used against you."

"Desiree, is that any way to speak about your great-grandmother?"

"Yes, ma'am, it's the truth," Desiree said.

"Oh hush. Like I was saying, Madison, your parents were never meant to be together. There was someone else your mother should have married. But then you would not have been born. Adrian is a good man. Don't let fear keep you from finding happiness."

The essence shimmered in the doorway to Desiree's office. A ghost was speaking to her, telling her she was acting a fool.

"Thank you, Eugenia," she said. "I'll take your words under consideration."

"Do more than that," she said. "Go get your man."

Desiree snickered. "But first, she's buying me dinner and you need to disappear. Here comes a guest."

The ghost vanished, but the smell of lavender remained.

"Come on, let's go eat. And you can update me on your fake dating."

"I'm never do it again," she said. "It hurts as bad as real dating when it ends."

Two hours later, she dropped Desiree off at the Burnett Ranch and began the long drive home.

Her phone rang and she saw it was Adrian. Why was he calling her? It was almost ten o'clock at night.

She didn't answer because she was driving. The road was dark and windy and she had to watch for deer.

When she pulled up in the parking lot of the apartment, she saw his truck sitting there.

He got out and met her at her car.

"Come on, we've got to go," he said. "I've been trying to reach you for two hours."

"What's wrong?"

"It's your mother. We need to get to the hospital. They took her by ambulance about seven o'clock this evening."

Fear spiraled through her and she ran to his truck. He helped her inside and then he sped down the road.

"I'm sorry. I was driving and I didn't want to answer while I was on that road from the Burnett's," she said.

He nodded.

"What happened with Mom," she asked. "She was at my house earlier today and she complained of feeling tired."

"She collapsed while she was making dinner. Blake found her on the kitchen floor and called 911."

Terror gripped her. She couldn't lose her mother. Not now. Not after everything with Adrian.

They reached the small hospital and they both jumped out of the truck and she ran inside with Adrian by her side.

The person at the desk advised that her mother was in the ER. In the waiting area, all of Adrian's brothers were sitting there, looking out of place. They all loved her mother and that warmed her heart. What would it be like to be a part of his family?

In some ways, they already were, but if she married Adrian, it would be official.

"We haven't heard a thing," Blake said, a worried expression on his face. "She's been back there several hours now."

"Let me see if I can find out anything," she said, walking up to a desk.

The nurse led her back to her mother and she grabbed Adrian's hand for him to come with her. The touch of his fingers wrapped in hers gave her strength, and she glanced at him. He still wore a worried expression.

"Mom," she cried rushing over to her.

"I'm all right," she said. "It wasn't another stroke. My blood work is not looking good and they're going to keep me overnight to stabilize me. I knew I was tired and not feeling good today."

Her mother glanced at Adrian by her side. "Sorry about dinner tonight."

"Susan, I don't give a damn about dinner. You scared us so bad. As long as you're all right, that's all that matters."

She smiled at him and then she gazed at her daughter.

"If something happens to me, you know where everything is right?"

Terror spiraled through Madison. She couldn't lose her mother, not now.

"Don't even say it. You're going to be fine. I'm sorry I wasn't here when they brought you in."

"It's all right. You were having dinner with Desiree," she said. "I'd forgotten until just now."

The nurse walked in. "Good news, we have a room ready for you. Let us get her transported up there and then you two can come in and say goodnight. She needs to rest."

Together, they walked out of the room and were greeted by his brothers.

"They're admitting her. It's not a stroke, but they want to run more tests and make certain her blood work is good," she told the men who all stared at her.

The guys relaxed and she couldn't help but reach out and pull them all in for a hug. "Thank you for taking good care of her."

"She's everything to us," Blake said.

"She's our second mother," Cody replied.

Dakota and Evan grinned. "We want to see her. We want to make certain she's really going to be all right."

Only Garth remained quiet, his face white with worry.

"They're going to move her to a room and then we'll all go up and see her," Adrian said. "But we can't stay long because she needs to rest."

Garth, the youngest, shook his head. "I think one of us should stay here and make certain she receives the care she needs."

This was the family she wanted around her. Not her stepsisters, stepmother, or father. These were the people who cared about her and her mother.

Glancing at Adrian, she decided she needed to be honest with him. As soon as they left the hospital, she would tell him her feelings.

Thirty minutes later, they all stood around her mother's bed, smiling at her and telling her to get better when the nurse came to the door.

"All right, folks, you've had a chance to tell her goodnight. It's time for me to take her vitals, give her some medication, and turn down the lights. Time for you to go home."

Madison leaned over, hugged her, and kissed her on the cheek. "I'll see you in the morning."

"Goodnight, sweetie," she said. "Remember what we talked about."

She nodded. Then the boys, one by one, hugged her goodnight.

When it came Adrian's turn, she reached up and kissed him on the cheek. "Goodnight."

They all left the hospital together and when they reached the parking lot, he glanced at her. "Do you want one of the other boys to take you home?"

"No, I want you," she said.

His brows rose and he opened the truck door for her and helped her inside.

They were silent on the way to her apartment. But when they pulled into the parking lot, she gazed at him. "Come up, we need to speak."

Once they were inside the door, she took off her coat, put her purse on the counter, and then she motioned for him to sit on the couch.

Sinking down beside him, she sighed. How did she tell him the reason she ran was because she had fallen in love with him?

"You know my family situation," she said. "After you left last week, my father called and demanded I give him money. I told him that you and I had broken up and he called me all kinds of names. Said I was the biggest fool. And in some ways, I have to agree with him."

Adrian shook his head. "You're not a fool."

"No, but I realized before the ball last week that I was falling in love with you. That you were the perfect man for me. We had fun, we laughed, we played, and that scared the hell out of me. I still believe that I'm not good marriage material because of who my father is. And yet, this week I've been so miserable without you. I've missed you. But you don't want to marry either."

He'd shown no reaction to her telling him that she was falling in love with him. None and that scared her. What if he didn't want her love or thought she was just another woman after his money?

"I'm not like the other women who were chasing after you. Your money is yours, not mine, and it never will be," she said, hoping he was going to respond to her declaration of love. What if she was the only one feeling this way?

He held up his hand. "Before that last ball, I knew things had changed between us. Remember, I even asked you why we couldn't continue to date and you refused."

"That's because my feelings were getting involved and I was so afraid."

He grinned. "Then after we stayed at that hotel for two of the best days of my life, I woke up and you were gone, and it about destroyed me. I've fallen so hard for you, Madison. I love you. I want to marry you. I want to have a family with you. You are the girl I should've been with all along, and I know deep in my heart that you're the right choice for me."

Tears filled her eyes. He loved her.

"These last two months, you've healed my wounded heart and made me believe in love again, and while I know that you're not ready to dance down the aisle with me, someday soon, I hope you'll be my wife. During my 'fake' engagement announcement was when I realized you are the woman I want to spend the rest of my life with."

He pulled her into his arms and she clung to him. "I'm so, so sorry I left you that day. Desiree gave me so much crap about leaving without speaking to you, but I was terrified. And then my father started texting me. I love you, Adrian. I love you so much, it frightens me."

"Me too," he said, holding her. "We'll take it slow. One day at a time. And when you're ready, we'll make it official. Our bogus dating and engagement have turned real and no one is going to come between us. No women pursuing me. No cheating. Nothing. Only you and me and the family I hope we someday create."

Standing, she pulled him up, took him by the hand, and led him to the bedroom.

"Tonight, we're going to celebrate the love we have for each other," she said, pulling his face down to hers.

"I love you, Madison," he whispered against her lips.

"I love you, Adrian."

CHAPTER 17

A month later, Adrian and Madison were horseback riding through the pasture in the spring air.

Susan was home from the hospital, and they had put her on new medication that they hoped would keep her out of the hospital.

The boys were busy moving cows to the farthest pastures to enjoy the new spring grass and getting cattle ready for market.

"Where are we going?" she asked him.

"What?" he asked her. "Can't we spend time together?"

The last month, they'd spent dating. Real dating. And in his pocket, he had a new piece of jewelry for her.

"There's the family oak tree," she said.

"Yes, ma'am," he replied, wondering if she'd guessed his intent.

They pulled their horses beneath the tree and he ground tethered both horses before he came around and helped her off.

"Adrian, what are we doing here?"

He grinned. She was getting suspicious. Gazing at her, he saw the fear on her face, but then he also saw something else. Something that he hoped was excitement.

Getting down on one knee, he pulled the ring box from his pocket. "I know we've done this once before, but this time I wanted to ask you to marry me beneath the family oak tree. The place my family believes is traditional and couples who come here last forever. You know I love you, Madison. You own my heart. Here, beneath this tree, I'm asking you to be my wife. To let me love you all the days you have on this earth. And I pledge to you that I will never cheat on you. You're the only woman for me."

He opened the ring box. "Will you marry me?"

A smile spread across her face and she launched herself into his arms. "Yes, I'll marry you. The sooner the better."

That surprised him.

"I mean it, Madison. We've both suffered from cheaters in our lives. I'm yours forever."

"And no one can tear me away from you," she said, kissing him on the lips. "I love you, Adrian. I can't wait to be your wife. And when I said the sooner the better, it's because we might have created a little bundle of joy in that hotel room."

Jaw hanging down, he stared at her.

"You're pregnant?"

"I think so," she said. "I've got all the signs and symptoms. And I've not had a period in almost two months."

Excitement filled him and he kissed her hard.

"I'm so thrilled. A wedding *and* we're going to start our family."

He took the ring out of the box and placed it on her finger. It was the same ring he'd given her during the fake engagement, but he'd had the jeweler add a special message on the inside of the band.

YOURS FOR REAL AND FOREVER.

"I love you, Madison. I can't wait to start our life together."

She reached up and stroked his face. "Me too, Adrian. Me too. I love you and I'm so excited about being your wife and this baby we're going to have."

Sweeping her into his arms, he grinned. "Let's go back and tell the family. I love you so much, Madison."

"I love you," she said grinning. "From fake dating to forever love."

"Forever," he said.

CHAPTER 18

Standing in the family room of the big house, Blake Landry stared at the letter in his hands. Who the hell had the nerve to send him this?

He read the missive once again.

Someone is keeping secrets from you. Someone you once loved has a child they don't want you to know about.

All right, maybe in his younger years he'd been a little wild. A little crazy. And he'd probably had too much to drink on several occasions, but he always used a condom. And he did his best to leave on good terms with every girl he'd broken up with.

So who was hiding something from him? And was it really his child? No, he would know if he had a child, wouldn't he?

Most of his past girlfriends lived here in town. Did any one of them have a child? And with the ranch's money now, he would figure someone would step forward and expect child support.

He wasn't certain this was real. Somebody was playing games and he didn't appreciate it. But still, what if it was true?

"Hey, Blake what are you doing?" Cody his younger brother asked.

He certainly didn't want his family to learn about this. There would be hell to pay if they learned he had a child that none of them knew about.

"Reading the mail," he said, standing in the kitchen.

"Did you hear that Adrian is taking Madison out to the family oak tree today?"

"Uh-huh," he said, knowing that his brother and Madison were right for one another. He'd seen the way they looked at each other, and he was happy for them. This time, he felt certain his brother had chosen wisely.

"You seem distracted," Cody said.

And he was. He was trying to determine which girlfriend was hiding a baby from him. There was no hint as to what the age of the child was. There was no other information.

"Excuse me," he said and walked out the door of the kitchen. He had to go back to his house and make a list.

Then, one by one, he was going to see each woman until he learned who was hiding his child from him.

When he reached the house, he had to search high and low for a piece of paper and a pen, but when he finished, twelve names were written down, but out of that number, eight were married. Surely, this woman wouldn't keep a secret like this from her husband, would she?

He would check out those first. Then he would move on to the last four who were single.

And if this message was true, when he learned who had kept this information from him, there would be hell to pay.

Available Everywhere!

. . .

THE
COWBOY
Billionaire's
FATE
USA Today Bestselling Author
SYLVIA
McDANIEL

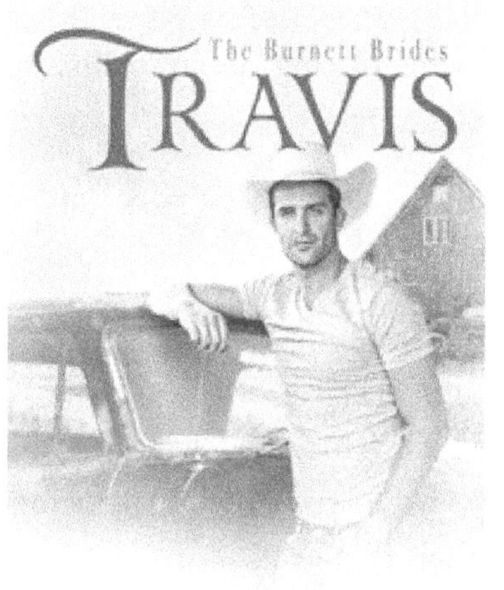

ravis Burnett glanced around the boardroom table at those gathered. It wasn't a fancy boardroom, but rather one filled with pictures of family members who had fought and struggled on the Burnett Ranch making it a success.

For over a century, they had worked cattle and made this outfit one of the most profitable and most lucrative in all of Texas.

Now twelve members all related to Eugenia and Thomas Burnett, who started the Burnett Ranch over one hundred years ago, sat around the table to make decisions about their commercial ranch. A dozen members who he often felt like throttling when they came before the board with their cocka-mamie ideas, who he knew many would disagree with his latest idea.

And still, he had to try. They had more than enough

money. Why not focus on the cattle and horses? Especially now that they were talking about reality television shows coming to the dude ranch.

Not a good idea.

"Why in the world would we want to let a ghost hunting show come to the ranch?" he asked, wondering what they were thinking. Or smoking for that matter. "We don't need that kind of notoriety."

Most of the board members were in their twenties, all family with only two of the previous generation still making decisions about their corporation.

"It could draw even more attention and make us even more popular," his cousin Joshua said.

The fool must not have been visited by their great-great-great-great-grandmother. All they needed was for the television show to see her, and oh yes, they would most definitely be the most popular dude ranch in the U.S.—for all the wrong reasons.

"Have you been visited by the ghost?" Travis asked. Was he the only one of this generation who had seen her?

"You don't believe that nonsense do you?" Joshua said, his smile wide. "Come on, ghosts are not real. And if they are, we should make money on them."

"Yeah, they need to earn their keep," his cousin Cody said laughing. "We could make a lot of money on this show, and think of the free advertising."

"Think of all the looky-loos we'd get. Spend the night at the ranch and see a ghost," he said.

"She's not real," Justin said. "Eugenia Burnett Jones lives on because of her matchmaking reputation."

"How do you think your ancestors found love?" Aunt Rose asked.

"Oh, please," Jacob said. "If she was the matchmaker, why aren't you married?"

Oh, dear, that was not the way to get along with their aunt. The woman could be vindictive if she felt you were not supporting the family business the way she thought you should.

"We'll talk after this is over. I thought you would have known my story, but I'll be sure to enlighten you," she said, her face red.

That kid had a lot to learn if he wanted to stay on the board and be in Aunt Rose's good graces.

What could he say that wouldn't make him look like a fool? And yet they needed to know. Maybe if he admitted to seeing her, others would as well.

"I've seen her," he said, not wanting to admit to it, but knowing that some apparition had visited him and told him it was past time for him to remarry. "I'll give her your name the next time she comes to visit."

The damn ghost bothered him about once a week telling him about the latest guests that she thought would be a good match for him. And so far, he'd avoided all of them.

His cousin Joshua leaned back in his chair and laughed. "I didn't think you visited the bars. Did you hold a seance like our ancestor used to do?"

"I only drink at home," he said. "And no seances were held. Just wait, she'll come visit you. Then let's talk."

The man shook his head, but everyone else at the table remained silent. They either had seen the ghost or they weren't saying. She'd been here for generations and even his father had confessed to seeing her.

"We don't need that kind of publicity," his aunt Rose said. "That could hurt our business."

The woman had never married, but rather made the ranch her permanent home and lived in the big house. Someday she would give it up, and Travis was next in line to live there.

But while the house had been remodeled, added onto, and made into a modern mansion, he would never move into the old homestead. A family needed to live in the house that had existed for over a hundred years. Since he never planned on marrying again, he would probably give it to his brother Tanner.

"Time to move on. I make a motion that we allow the ghost-hunting television show be allowed to film on the ranch," his cousin Jacob said, glancing at his brother Joshua with a grin.

"All in favor vote," Rose said. She was the head of the family and the corporation. Nothing got by this woman.

Only four of the twelve voted to allow them to film on the ranch. Travis smiled and decided it was time for him to make his desires known. It was time they realized what a pain in the ass the dude ranch had become.

He was tired of drunken guests, crying children, people ignoring the rules, and women who only came to go shopping in Dallas. People could be a real pain in the ass and so many that were sitting around this board didn't have to deal with them.

"Motion failed," Rose said, the oldest of the family there and the head of the directors. "The next item on the agenda is from Travis."

She gazed at him like he was the biggest pain in the ass of the group, but he knew that wasn't true. That was his cousin Cameron. That boy had tried the patience of all of them with his privileged behavior. Travis had taken his Corvette keys away twice and told him if it happened a third time, he'd take the car.

No one was allowed to drive drunk and Cameron did enjoy his beer.

All of their eyes were on him, wondering what he wanted this time. And they were going to be shocked.

"I'd like to make a motion that we close the dude ranch part of the business," he said.

They all stared at him like he was crazy. Several of his cousins leaned back in their chairs and laughed. Of course, they were the ones who did not work with the people. They were the ones who didn't have to put up with some of the stunts their guests had pulled.

"Why?" Rose, who was nearing seventy, asked. "We make good money from the dude ranch."

"Because I'm tired of dealing with the crazies who come here thinking they can be vacation cowboys. Someone is going to get seriously hurt and then we'll be sued."

"We have insurance to handle that," Aunt Rose said.

Justin shook his head. Travis's father, Mark Burnett, had taken the ranch into the modern day and upgraded their operations. But still, that didn't mean they needed the dude ranch. They were all extremely rich from the family business. Almost every Burnett had over a billion dollars in the bank thanks to their hard-working ancestors, great cattle, and even a little oil money.

His cousin Caleb shook his head. The boy had graduated

college with a marketing degree and his focus was on getting them as much publicity as possible with a fancy website, newsletters, and Instagram and Facebook profiles. Not to mention the money he spent on advertising.

"I'm with Rose. Our profit margin is over fifty percent. People come here and enjoy riding horses, swimming, and our cookouts. We're in almost every travel magazine in the state of Texas and I'm attending a travel show next week in Washington D.C. that will showcase us even more."

Damn, this was not going well.

"Caleb, I'm glad you've made the dude ranch a big success, but I'm the one who has to deal with entertaining our guests and making certain that our clients don't do something stupid like try to tame a bull. That happened last year."

A smile crossed his cousin's face. "And you do a fine job of it. But we spent over twenty thousand dollars to get into these travel magazines. That would be a complete waste of money. I don't like to squander money."

Shit, this wasn't going well at all.

"Maybe, Travis, you should let the workers we hire do the trail rides and even the rodeo we host," Cody Burnett, Caleb's brother said.

Now that was just pure craziness. Neither one of them had ever worked the guest angle of the dude ranch.

"You would entrust our guests' safety to hired hands? Are you willing to risk us being sued?"

His brother Tucker who had been leaning back watching the interplay between the family finally spoke up. "I'm with Travis. Our guests need to be protected from themselves. That must always be something a family member handles. And a priority."

Oh, dear, his aunt Rose was frowning and she had that look on her face that implied you were suggesting they hire monsters. This was not someone you wanted to piss off and it appeared that Travis had just made her furious.

"The Burnett Ranch was established in 1870 right after the Civil War. My grandfather opened the dude ranch back in 1946 and saved our heritage with the money he made showing city slickers our life in the country. I'm never going to be for closing a piece of our heritage," his aunt Rose said, glaring at him like he was robbing the family silver.

The old woman had more money than any of them and no heirs.

"You're so right," his cousin Desiree said and Travis wanted to barf.

The woman worked in the front office and didn't know a thing about ranch life, though her father had been a great cowboy until an accident sidelined him. Now he sat on the board, but hardly ever said anything. He just let the younger generation make the decisions with Aunt Rose leading them.

"Any other discussion on closing the dude ranch?"

Everyone was silent.

"Let's vote," his aunt said.

There was no chance in hell this was going to pass, but he had to try for his own sanity.

"There are only three votes. The dude ranch will continue," his aunt said. "Next piece of business is the hiring of the new chef. She graduated from Escoffier in Boulder, Colorado, and is top rated."

Tanner raised his brows. "So why is she willing to come to a ranch on the outskirts of Texas? What have we got to offer? Why not some fancy-schmancy restaurant in New York?"

His aunt smiled. "Let's just say that she's had some bad things happen in her life and she needs a break from the hifalutin culinary world but wants to continue doing what she loves."

"Well, then she's not going to stay here long," Tanner said.

Travis remembered when she had flown down and toured their kitchen and cooked them a meal. The food had been excellent. Kind of frou-frou, but that's what people were expecting.

"Stop making assumptions, Tanner," Cousin Cameron said. "We don't know that. She may learn she loves Texas."

"No snow, warm winters, and hot-as-hell summers," Justin said.

Travis glanced at his brother and grinned. He'd just gotten his hand slapped by the next to youngest Burnett cousin Cameron and a smackdown from Justin. Desiree was the youngest, but that girl had a head on her shoulders.

"I make a motion that we hire her," Cousin Desiree said.

"Have we tasted her cooking?" Tucker asked.

"Yeah, we had her out here a few weeks ago. You were in LA," Cody said.

That was the problem with Tucker. He had his own business to run and, oftentimes, he wasn't here when important decisions were made, though he did his best to attend every board meeting.

"Where was I?" Tanner asked.

Travis leaned over. "You were getting a checkup at the VA Hospital in Dallas," he said.

Tanner frowned and Travis knew he didn't like it when they talked about his PTSD. But the man had come so far from when he came home from the war.

"All in favor, raise your hands," his aunt said.

It was unanimous.

"She's hired. I'll have Katie send her the package offer. If all goes well, she'll soon be here."

They all glanced around at each other knowing the board meeting was almost over and ready to get out of here. The small room was stuffy and he could hear the office staff right outside the doors keeping things running.

"I need someone to make a motion to adjourn the meeting."

His cousin Jacob spoke up and immediately they all voted on ending their once-a-month board meeting.

Once it was over, Travis slowly rose, knowing what he had to go do. It was past time and he wanted to get out there before they closed the gates.

"Gotta go," he told his family and grabbed his hat on the way out the door.

Shoving it on his head, he walked out to his truck parked not far from the office building.

Climbing in, he started up the vehicle and pulled out of the drive. As much as he hated cemeteries, he seemed to always find a sense of desolate peace when visiting.

It took him about twenty minutes to drive to the Riverdale Cemetery. When he pulled through the gate, the memory of the day of the funeral slapped him in the face.

Of standing between his brothers, staring in horror as they lowered her casket into the ground. The feeling of numbness that this couldn't be happening had overwhelmed him. In an instant, his life had changed forever.

Putting the truck in park and turning off the ignition, he

reached for the flowers he'd bought and grabbed them off the seat.

As he climbed out of the truck, he glanced around at the barren place and the sense of sadness that seemed to permeate the air.

Walking up to the grave, he stared down at the tombstone. *Amanda Burnett and child. Taken Much Too Soon.*

With a sigh, he leaned down and took out the old flowers in the vase and put the new ones in. Every time he came here, his heart would ache with loneliness. Sorrow would fill his eyes with tears.

"God, how I still miss you. Our baby would be almost two years old. You two were my life and now I have nothing."

The wind blew and he heard the tinkling of wind chimes. It almost sounded like she answered him.

"I doubt you know I'm here, but still I have to come check on you. Even if I'm just staring at a piece of rock with your name on it."

Slowly he rose. "Today, I tried to convince the family to close the dude ranch, but they weren't interested. I couldn't help but think about how much you loved the talent show. Without your touch, it's just never the same. God, how do I go on living without you?"

For almost three years, he'd asked himself that same question over and over.

He sighed and glanced around at all the tombstones. His heart ached with the sadness of this lonely land. Glancing over, he saw other family members, but he never thought to bring flowers to them.

Only Amanda and their baby.

Swallowing hard, he knew he had to leave. He couldn't stay long, it hurt too much.

"Gotta go, darling. See you next time."

Turning, he hurried to the truck, jumped in, and started the vehicle.

Damn, it just wasn't fair. They had loved each other since they were sixteen and their life together had ended way too early.

Available Everywhere!

Contemporary Romance
Burnett Brides Contemporary Times
Travis
Tanner
Tucker
Joshua
Jacob
Justin
Cameron
Caleb
Cody
Desiree
Burnett Brides Contemporary Box Set Books 5-7
Burnett Brides Contemporary Box Set 8-10
Burnett Brides Contemporary Box Set 11-14

Return to Cupid, Texas
Cupid Stupid
Cupid Scores
Cupid's Dance
Cupid Help Me!
Cupid Cures
**Cupid's Heart
Cupid Santa
**Cupid Second Chance
Cupid Charmer
Cupid Crazy
Cupid's Bachelorette
Cupid Games
Return to Cupid Box Set Books 1-3

Cupid Help Me Box Set Books 4-6
Return to Cupid Box Set Books 7-9
Return to Cupid Box Set Books 10-12
**The Unlucky Bride

Contemporary Romance
My Sister's Boyfriend
The Wanted Bride
The Reluctant Santa
The Relationship Coach
Secrets, Lies, & Online Dating

Bride, Texas Multi-Author Series
**The Unlucky Bride

Coming Home for Christmas
I'll Be Home for Christmas
White Christmas
Santa's Baby
All I Want For Christmas
Box Set

Inheriting An Irish Groom
Inheriting a Scottish Castle

Kissing Oaks Billionaire Brothers
The Cowboy Billionaire's Lucky Break
The Cowboy Billionaire's Fate
The Cowboy Billionaire's Playbook
The Cowboy Billionaire's Secret
The Cowboy Billionaire's Deception

The Cowboy Billionaire's Match
Kissing Oaks Billionaire Brothers Box Set 1-3
Kissing Oaks Billionaire Brothers Box Set 4-6

Lipstick and Lead 2.0
Nailing the Hit Man
Nailing the Billionaire
Nailing the Single Dad
Box Set

Secrets of Mustang Island
Secrets of a Summer Place
Secrets of a Runaway Bride
Secrets From the Past
Secrets of a Reckless Life
Secrets of a Hidden Life
Secrets of a Midnight Letter

Secrets of Mustang Island Novellas
The Summer I Loved You
When We Meet Again
Christmas at Mustang Island

The Langley Legacy
Collin's Challenge

Short Sexy Reads
Racy Reunions Series
Paying For the Past
My Christmas Soldier
Cupid's Revenge

Western Historicals
A Hero's Heart
Second Chance Cowboy
Ethan

American Brides
**Katie: Bride of Virginia

Angel Creek Christmas Brides
**Charity
**Ginger
**Minne
**Cora
Angel Creek Christmas Box Set

Bad Girls of the West
Scandalous Sadie
Ravenous Rose
Tempting Tessa
Nellie's Redemption
Bad Girls Box Set

The Burnett Brides Series
The Rancher Takes A Bride
The Outlaw Takes A Bride
The Marshal Takes A Bride
The Christmas Bride
Boxed Set

Lipstick and Lead Series
Desperate

Deadly
Dangerous
Daring
Determined
Deceived
Defiant
Devious
Lipstick and Lead Box Set Books 1-4
Lipstick and Lead Box Set Books 5-9
Lipstick and Lead Box Set Books 1-9
**Quinlan's Quest

Mail Order Bride Tales
**A Brother's Betrayal
**Pearl
**Ace's Bride

Scandalous Suffragettes of the West
**Abigail
Bella
Mistletoe Scandal

Southern Historical Romance
A Scarlet Bride

The Cuvier Women
Wronged
Betrayed
Beguiled
Boxed Set

The Debutante's of Durango
The Debutante's Scandal
The Debutante's Gamble
The Debutante's Revenge
The Debutante's Santa
Box Set

**** Denotes a sweet book.**

**Want to learn about my new releases before anyone else?
Sign up for my New Book Alert and receive a
complimentary book.**

Sylvia McDaniel is a USA Today Bestselling author with over one hundred western historical and contemporary romance novels under her belt. Known for creating memorable bad boys and good girls who can't help getting into trouble, she spends her days weaving compelling tales filled with heart, humor, and unexpected plot twists. Her family-oriented stories have earned her a loyal fanbase, and she's always dreaming up new ways to keep her readers turning the page.

Married to her best friend for over thirty years, Sylvia lives in Colorado, where she enjoys hiking and taking in the natural beauty of the forest that borders their home. Their spoiled dachshund, Zeus (who has his own column in her newsletter), and brat dog Bailey keeps them company on their adventures.

Sylvia keeps close ties to her southern roots, especially when it comes to football. A dedicated fan of both the Denver Broncos and the Dallas Cowboys, she's happiest when they're winning.

Love books? Love deals? Love a little mischief? Sign up for my Substack—it's free!
https://sylviamcdanielauthor.substack.com/
The End